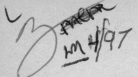

"I now pronounce you— no, wait!

"The rings. Do you have the rings?" The Wedding Chapel's officiant looked anxious. Or as anxious as a man dressed in a toreador outfit could look.

"Lord, I forgot all about that," Nick muttered.

But their witness, an elderly man in jogging shorts, sprang into action. "Rings—" he announced, flashing open a leather case. "Take your pick—all kinds, all sizes."

It was a wonderful and bewildering array, but Lindy chose a simple gold band, and Nick found one to match.

The toreador slapped his book shut, giving a final flourish of his cape. "I now pronounce you husband and wife!"

"Hey, aren't you forgetting something?" Nick demanded.

The toreador opened his book again and peered anxiously inside it. "Oh, yes. You may now kiss the bride."

Dear Reader,

I'm delighted to be part of Harlequin Romance's Bridal Collection. Not only was writing this book a treat for me, but it also gave me a chance to remember my own wedding over fifteen years ago. It seemed that if anything could go wrong that day, it did. My family and my fiancé weren't on speaking terms, the preacher never *stopped* speaking (although I can't for the life of me remember a word he said), the cake was late, the music was flat, I had too many flower girls and not enough flowers, and right before the procession, the entire wedding party got the giggles. It's no surprise, then, that I think weddings are most romantic when nothing goes quite right—and, in the end, two exhausted newlyweds escape on their well-deserved honeymoon. But perhaps the most romantic way of all to get married is . . . eloping! My secret fantasy is someday my husband and I will run off together and renew our vows in a Las Vegas wedding chapel.

Meanwhile, I hope you enjoy the story of Nick and Lindy. Thank you for allowing me to share it with you.

Sincerely,

Ellen James

LOVE YOUR ENEMY
Ellen James

Harlequin Books

TORONTO • NEW YORK • LONDON
AMSTERDAM • PARIS • SYDNEY • HAMBURG
STOCKHOLM • ATHENS • TOKYO • MILAN
MADRID • WARSAW • BUDAPEST • AUCKLAND

ISBN 0-373-03202-1

Harlequin Romance first edition June 1992

LOVE YOUR ENEMY

CHAPTER ONE

LINDY MACALLISTER rattled the doorknob of the trailer. Darn it, she knew the wretched man was in there somewhere; his truck was parked a few yards away next to a juniper tree. Lindy glanced at her watch. It was almost seven in the morning. She'd already spent an hour out on the mesa, standing guard over her little owls. But there was really only one way to protect the owls. She had to confront Nick Jarrett—confront him and stop what he was doing before it was too late!

Lindy knocked on the door one more time, then started prowling around the trailer to peer through the windows. Hammersmith loped close at her heels, almost tripping her. Even though Hammersmith was a huge dog, with big, fuzzy yellow paws, he was still as exuberant as a puppy. This morning he'd chased joyously after owls and jackrabbits until Lindy had confined him to the car. Now he bumped against her and licked her hand with intense thoroughness, as if to thank her for allowing him his freedom again.

"Calm down, Hammers. Remember, you're on probation. I expect the very best behavior from you." Lindy patted the dog's head with easy affection. Advancing on another of the trailer's windows, she pressed her nose against the glass and stared hard. She

saw a man fast asleep on a sofa, his shoes, jacket and
tie strewn carelessly on the floor around him. So this
was the mighty Nick Jarrett—her newest adversary in
the battle she'd been waging for months with Aldridge Aviation. He had a rangy build and was too
long for the couch, his legs dangling over the edge. His
arms were flung out, as if opened wide to greet someone in his dreams. Lindy tapped on the pane and he
began to stir, yawning expansively until she could see
a whole set of solid white teeth. Then he stretched,
rolled over—and tumbled to the floor with a thud that
reverberated clear through to the window.

It was an impressive tumble, it really was. Lindy
would've liked to see it replayed in slow motion. But
already the man was sitting up, the sound of his curses
only slightly muffled. Lindy tapped on the window
again.

"Who the devil are you?" he bellowed.

"Jarrett? Nick Jarrett?" she called back. "Why
don't you let me in? Then we can talk."

He didn't move. He frowned at her as he sat there
on the floor, his knees jutting up at odd angles. Lindy
adjusted the brim of her battered Dodgers baseball cap
and gave him a critical perusal. He was attractive in
spite of that sour expression on his face—blue eyes
and light brown hair with startling glints of gold. His
hair had been neatly trimmed at one time, that much
was apparent, but now it was shaggy from growing
out. His dark trousers were expensive yet thoroughly
wrinkled, and the well-tailored effect of his shirt was
ruined because the collar was twisted awry. Everything about him gave the same impression: sophisti-
cation and polish suffering a rapid onslaught of chaos.

He reminded Lindy of an elegant house that needed its front lawn mowed.

"Go away," he said, mouthing the words in exaggerated fashion, as if he thought she couldn't hear him through the window.

"Let me in," she mouthed right back. Goodness, the man looked ill-tempered; maybe he wasn't a morning person. Lindy drew her eyebrows together. She thoroughly disapproved of late risers. Now she had one more reason to detest Jarrett and his miserable company, Aldridge Aviation.

He stood, heading toward the front door. The instant the door swung open, Hammersmith gamboled up the steps of the trailer and flung himself straight at Nick Jarrett like a big yellow torpedo.

"What in tarnation...!" The rest of Jarrett's exclamation was garbled, for Hammersmith's tongue had an impressive reach.

"Oh, dear," Lindy murmured. This wasn't exactly what she'd had in mind when it came to confronting Nick Jarrett. She had no choice but to crowd into the trailer herself. "Down, Hammers. Down!" She tried to grab his collar, but he bounded into the living room. Lindy hurried after him, dismayed by the trail of muddy paw prints he was leaving on the pristine beige carpet. As discreetly as possible, she rubbed the sole of her hiking boot over one of the tracks. That only smeared the mud deeper into the carpet.

Jarrett scowled at Lindy from the doorway. "Do you mind telling me who the heck you are? And why the heck you unleashed that crazed mutt in here?"

At last she had a firm grip on Hammersmith's collar, but she could feel her face burning with embarrassment. Two muddy paw prints adorned the front of Nick Jarrett's expensive shirt. Lindy almost lifted her hand to dab at the mud on his broad chest, but somehow that didn't seem appropriate.

"Um, well, Mr. Jarrett, Hammersmith hates being locked in the car, and I started to feel sorry for him. You know how it is...."

Jarrett's implacable expression conveyed that he didn't know how it was at all. She tried again.

"Believe it or not, I *have* had quite a bit of success training Hammers to obey me. He backslides now and then, that's the problem. Why don't I just put him out, and then you and I can get down to business." Lindy tugged on Hammersmith's collar. "Come on, boy. You'll have to wait for me outside."

The dog wouldn't budge. He stared at Lindy with mournful, accusing brown eyes. She tugged harder, and then she started pushing his rear end. Hammersmith dug his paws into the carpet, making muddy skid marks all the way to the door. Jarrett stepped back and watched this procedure without saying a word. Lindy slammed the door shut before Hammersmith could turn around and come rollicking into the trailer again. She gave Jarrett what she hoped was a brisk, professional nod.

"There. That's taken care of. You have to understand, Hammersmith hasn't known proper care and discipline all his life. I could tell he'd been a stray for a long time when I found him. You'd be amazed at the progress he's made since then. Honestly, you would be." She winced at the expressive whines coming from the other side of the door.

Nick Jarrett rubbed both hands through his hair. "Maybe I'm still asleep, and you and your mutt are part of some cockeyed nightmare I'm having. Is that too much to hope?"

Hammersmith howled as if in agony. Lindy did her best to ignore him. She positioned her feet strategically over as many paw prints as possible. It was no use; those muddy prints frolicked their way all through the living room. Jarrett gazed at them sardonically.

Lindy cleared her throat. "Well, now. I can clean things up in a flash, and you'll never know Hammers was here. Do you have a broom I could use, or a vacuum, or...something?" She paused. Her housekeeping skills were not the best, and she wasn't sure exactly what device would do the job with this mess.

"Forget it," Jarrett said after a moment, surveying the muddy smears on his shirt. "Just get your dog off my stoop before he learns how to sing opera. We'll consider ourselves even."

Hammersmith moaned from the other side of the door. Lindy decided it was time to plunge ahead with the reason she was there. "Mr. Jarrett, I'm glad I can finally speak to someone from Aldridge Aviation—face-to-face. I'm tired of writing letters and making phone calls where no one listens to me. Maybe I can get some results now that you're here. The way I understand it, you're one of the partners in the company. The secretary in your St. Louis office said you'd decided to supervise this project personally."

"Yeah, right. So here I am in the exciting metropolis of Santiago, New Mexico." He picked up his jacket from the floor and tossed it onto the sofa, where it lay more rumpled than ever. "Let me guess.

You're the welcoming committee in this godforsaken town. How lucky could I get?''

"Welcoming you is the last thing on my mind! I'm Linden MacAllister." She waited for a response, but his face was blank. "They told you about me, didn't they?" she demanded. "I spoke to dozens of people in St. Louis, and—"

"Look, I've never heard of you, all right? Come back some other time, after I'm settled in. Maybe in a week or two. Make that a month."

"Oh, no. You're not getting rid of me that easily." She planted herself in the center of the room. "I've had enough of you Aldridge Aviation people telling me you'll listen later. I'm staying right here until you talk to me about the owls!"

"Why would I want to talk to you about owls?" He seemed genuinely puzzled.

"I'll tell you why." She took a deep breath. "Mr. Jarrett, out there on the mesa is a colony of burrowing owls fighting for its very existence. You see, the owls live right where you plan to build your new airplane factory. So you'll have to change your location and build somewhere else." The words spilled out of her on a tide of emotion. Usually Lindy was a matter-of-fact sort of person. But she'd come to love those little owls; she'd spent hour after hour watching them and learning their habits. They'd given her so much enjoyment, and now it was her turn to give something back. No bulldozers were going to threaten them or destroy their homes!

Nick stared at the door as Hammersmith's whines broadened in range and eloquence. "I don't believe it," he muttered. "I land in this dinky town, and first thing I know some birdbrained lady barges in here with a loony dog and starts ranting about owls. What next?''

Lindy's blood simmered. ''Mr. Jarrett, you can't just dismiss me as a crazy person. I'm not a problem that will go away. Trust me on that. You'll have to deal with me, whether you like it or not.''

He groaned, rubbing his head some more. ''I'm not talking about anything until I have at least four cups of coffee. Make that five.'' He strode into the kitchen and began poking around in the drawers and cupboards. ''This place was supposed to be stocked with food, dammit. Where's the coffee?'' He yanked open the cabinet under the sink and bent down to scowl at the pipes.

Just as Lindy had thought—he was a late riser. His craving for caffeine was an unmistakable sign. She crossed to lean against one of the counters so she could watch him banging through cupboards. His gold-brown hair was so frazzled it stood up like a crest of feathers, but somehow that only contributed to his image as a powerful executive. At last he found his coffee. He dumped some into a mug, not bothering to heat any water; he made do with the hot-water faucet at the sink. Lindy shuddered, and supposed she ought to be grateful he wasn't spooning coffee into his mouth straight from the can.

Nick sat down at a flimsy table that looked like it belonged in a dollhouse. His tall, broad-shouldered frame dwarfed the table even further, so it seemed as if he truly had stumbled into a house several sizes too small for him. Lindy felt a smile beginning, but she controlled herself. She couldn't afford to weaken where Nick Jarrett was concerned.

She marched to the table and plunked down her big purse. She used a little too much force and the purse toppled over, rocks and dirt spewing out of it. Nick grabbed his coffee mug just in time.

"Do you always carry a supply of rocks in your purse?"

Lindy flushed. This meeting was *not* proceeding as she'd planned. Something about Nick Jarrett made her feel awkward and unsure. She began scooping her treasures back into her purse where they belonged. Geology was her passion. Wherever she went, she would scan the ground for that one special rock she couldn't live without. Now her hand lingered on a good piece of quartz she'd discovered the other day; she loved its smooth, serene texture. She held the rock out to Nick. "Here. Rub your fingers over this a few times. It will do wonders for you. It's very relaxing, and much better for your metabolism than drinking coffee."

"You really *are* crazy," he muttered, but he allowed her to drop the glassy white quartz onto his palm. He gazed down at it with a skeptical expression. Lindy sat across from him.

"They must have told you something about me in St. Louis. I finally got through to your partner—Juliet Aldridge herself. She said she'd give you the file with all the letters I've written. Of course, she did clap the phone down in my ear. She seems like an awfully volatile person. I hope you're more reasonable than she is, I really do."

"Great. Wonderful. Just who I wanted to think about. Juliet." He pronounced the name forcefully, so that it came out "Joo-lee-ET." He sounded angry and disgusted. Maybe that was a good sign. Maybe he didn't get along with Juliet Aldridge, and so would be willing to fight her to protect the owls.

He bounced the quartz up and down on his palm, lost in his own thoughts. Lindy studied him. She sat perfectly still, the way she did when she was in the mountains or on the mesa and wanted to observe some wild creature at close range. There was a sense of the untamable about Nick Jarrett; after all her years in the outdoors, she recognized it instantly. His features were bold and uneven, with a shadow of a beard along his jaw. In spite of the wrinkled fabric of his shirt, Lindy could tell he had a strongly muscled body. And even though clumps of his hair were sticking straight up, he possessed an elegance as natural as that of a lion or leopard. He was a compelling man.

Lindy struggled to resist his attractiveness. She'd often asked herself why she liked rocks more than she liked men. And the answer was always the same: rocks were solid, dependable. She could take one look at a rock and know what it was made of. Shale and sandstone, hornblende and garnet and feldspar—she could count on them to be exactly what they appeared. But the men she'd known in her career could be treacherous, masking their true selves whenever it suited them. It hadn't been easy for Lindy to succeed as a geologic engineer, taking on a profession that was still a male province. She'd had to battle prejudice, jealousy, suspicion, ridicule and, worst of all, betrayal. She'd learned to protect her feelings, become as hard and implacable as granite itself!

So why was her skin tingling as she sat here across from Nick Jarrett? She yanked off her cap and fanned herself with the brim. Her black hair fell loose around her shoulders. Nick glanced over at her, glanced away... then slowly focused on her again.

"What do you know, there *is* a woman under there," he said in mock surprise. Lindy tried to look away from him but couldn't. His eyes were as clear and brilliant in color as a desert sky. She was suddenly too conscious of herself—her baggy trousers, her cotton work shirt, which disguised any feminine curves. What did Nick Jarrett see when he looked at her? A woman of muted earth shades, nothing to dazzle him? She did have healthy hair, dark and glossy as anthracite coal. It was nothing spectacular, perhaps, but she shampooed it every day and that had to be worth something. Gray eyes, a decisive nose that wasn't really too big, olive-toned skin... Lindy gave up. She was used to seeing details in nature, not in herself. It had been a long while since she'd cared what a man thought of her. Why did she care now?

"Hmm," Nick murmured, lapsing into silence once more as he regarded her. She squashed the crown of her baseball cap and then punched it back into shape. "What are you looking at?" she exclaimed. "Did I spill rhubarb jam all over myself?" She glanced down at the front of her shirt just to check.

"You had rhubarb for breakfast?" He made it sound like she'd been eating snakes or something equally revolting.

"Rhubarb jam on toast," she said. "All right, maybe it was more like rhubarb sauce. But it was delicious. My own recipe, by the way."

Nick jiggled the piece of quartz a few more times. Lindy noticed that he gave the rock a quick experimental rub before tossing it onto the table. She retrieved it, curling her fingers around its warmth. Actually the warmth belonged to Nick; he'd heated the quartz with his touch. Lindy shoved it hurriedly into one of the deep pockets of her canvas trousers. She needed to concentrate on the reason she'd come here—to stop Aldridge Aviation from hurting the owls. Nothing else mattered.

"You have to look at the file Juliet Aldridge gave you," she persisted. "I'm sure she gave you a file with my letters. Of course, I can always show you my copies." She started delving into her purse.

"Hold on." He frowned at her purse as if expecting some creature—perhaps an owl—to come hopping out of it. "Juliet dumped a whole confounded stack of paperwork on me. I'll look through that if it'll make you stop pestering me."

"It would be a step in the right direction," she conceded.

He scraped his chair away from the table and strode out of the room, grumbling under his breath. A few moments later he returned with a briefcase, still grumbling. He sounded like the aftershocks of an earthquake. Lindy couldn't make out what he was saying except for occasional words like "nonsensical" and "booby hatch" and "damn fool woman." She wondered if he was referring to her or to Juliet Aldridge—it was impossible to tell.

Nick slid his briefcase onto the table, edging her purse out of the way. Lindy didn't find this acceptable. Using her purse as a sort of battering ram, she pushed at his briefcase. Nick pushed back. The purse and the briefcase jockeyed for position, and meanwhile the poor table wobbled as if confused. Finally a precarious balance was achieved. Giving Lindy an acid look, Nick sat down and flipped open the briefcase. He pulled out one file after another.

"What the heck is all this stuff? I told Juliet to keep these witless report forms to herself. She knows I won't fill them out. Ah, here it is. MacAllister, L., just like you said." He sent another sour glance at Lindy, then leaned back in his chair to peruse the file. "Interesting. It says here you're Linden *Eloise* MacAllister, age twenty-eight, born in Albuquerque, New Mexico—"

"Wait! You're supposed to have my letters in there, nothing else. I never told anyone my middle name."

"What's the matter? Don't you like being called Eloise?"

She hated the name, positively hated it. But she tried not to let that show. "What else does it say about me? Hand that over." She made a grab for the file, but Nick held it out of reach. He seemed to be enjoying himself now. "This is company property. It's marked confidential, in fact. Says here you studied geology and engineering at Northwestern University. Not bad, not bad at all. I'm impressed, Eloise."

"Blast it, don't call me that. Someone's invaded my privacy. It's no business of Aldridge Aviation's where I went to school, or where I was born—or anything.

What's wrong with you people? You have spies scurrying around everywhere, is that it?''

He leaned back more comfortably, his spindly chair creaking in protest. "I wouldn't be surprised at anything Juliet does. She's thorough, that's for sure. Don't you want to know what else it says?"

Lindy made one more attempt to snatch the file out of his hand. He dodged her easily. "Very well, read the rest of it," she sighed. "Every bit."

He did go on reading the file—but only to himself, chuckling as he scanned the pages. Lindy tapped her fingers on the table, ready to explode. Then she saw a furry yellow head bounce up at the window. It disappeared, only to spring into view again a moment later. Boing...boing...boing! Up and down went Hammersmith's head, ears flying. He looked like he'd gotten hold of a pogo stick.

Lindy pursed her lips, not quite sure what to do next. Catching the direction of her gaze, Nick glanced over at the window. It was innocently blank. Just as Nick glanced away, however, the yellow head vaulted into the air and sailed back down out of sight.

Nick rattled the papers in the file folder. Again he looked sharply at the blank window. Shrugging, he returned to the file. Hammersmith's fuzzy yellow head popped up hopefully.

Nick frowned at the file folder. Down went the yellow head, up again—and this time Nick slapped the file folder onto the table and stared straight at Hammersmith. Both man and dog seemed perplexed at this sudden meeting of the eyes. Hammersmith's ears floated in the air like two question marks before disappearing from view.

Lindy inched her hand toward the file folder, but Nick grabbed it. "No, you don't," he said grimly. He went on staring out the window. "Good Lord," he muttered, shaking his head. "It's like watching a canine basketball."

Lindy turned her own chair resolutely away from the window. She didn't intend to encourage Hammersmith; he'd already caused enough trouble today. "What else does it say about me in there?" she asked. "I want to know everything. It's only fair."

It took Nick a few moments to drag his attention from the window, but at last he swiveled around and opened the folder again. "All right, all right... Turns out you're a college teacher. Professor MacAllister, a.k.a. Professor Mac. I like the sound of that. And this is a mouthful. You teach geologic and environmental engineering at the Chamberlin Institute of Technology. Not only that, but you're quite in demand as a consultant. This is definitely impressive. What else... You buy most of your clothes at army-surplus stores, and at least two times a week you treat yourself to a scoop of triple-fudge-banana-swirl frozen yogurt. Sounds like you have quite a sweet tooth, Professor Mac." He scanned the rest of the file. "That's about it. No prior subversive activities, no arrests, no boyfriend..."

Lindy gripped her purse with both hands. "This is going way too far. My private life is no concern of yours. No concern at all!"

Nick gave her an engaging smile. "Hey, I'm only telling you what it says here. But I think it's good we're getting to know each other, don't you? In fact, you should tell me more about yourself, especially the 'no boyfriend' part.''

Lindy didn't care to have Nick Jarrett probing below the surface of her life, like a chisel working its way under a layer of stone. She wished she'd never asked what was in that ridiculous file folder. ''I refuse to talk about something that's my own personal business,'' she declared. She was relieved when Nick glanced out the window and was distracted by Hammersmith again.

''Lord, the mutt's still at it out there, springing up and down like a deranged grasshopper. How long can he keep it up?''

''We could time him, if you'd like. I have a stopwatch on me. The way I see it, you never know when you might need a stopwatch. This is a case in point.'' Lindy started poking around in her purse again, but Nick wouldn't leave her in peace. Just the way he looked at her sent an odd, quivering warmth all through her body.

''Let's talk about you, Professor Mac. That's the only subject I'm really interested in right now.'' His voice was lazy and teasing, his eyes holding a glint of humor. ''So tell me. Exactly why is it you don't have a boyfriend?''

CHAPTER TWO

LINDY NEEDED A ROCK. Nick Jarrett's vibrant masculinity made her feel so warm and unsteady she feared she might be undergoing some sort of thermal stress. She dug into her trouser pocket and took out the piece of quartz. Rubbing her fingers over it, she regained a little equanimity.

"In answer to your question, I don't need a boyfriend. That's all there is to it. Simple as can be."

Nick didn't say anything. He merely went on regarding her with amusement. Lindy rubbed her quartz with more vigor, but that didn't stop her from feeling defensive, as if she had to justify her position to Nick.

"Look, it's not as if I haven't tried men. I was almost married once. And then—" Lindy clamped her mouth shut before more words could slip out. She saw the unmistakable pity on Nick's face. Oh, blast! She wouldn't tolerate pity from him or any man.

"It was all over a long time ago," she said, keeping her voice brisk. "I was lucky to find out what the Cluny was like before I married him. I'm very grateful for that."

Nick looked puzzled. "The Cluny? That's what you call him?"

Lindy shifted uneasily in her chair. She seemed to be blurting out all sorts of things this morning. "Well, what am I supposed to call Donald Cluny? I can't very well go around saying 'the jerk' or 'the creep.'"

"I get it," Nick murmured. "You've come up with a new kind of insult. Suppose some guy cuts you off in traffic. You can just yell, 'Hey, you Cluny!' I like the sound of that."

Lindy glared at him. "Are you finished?"

"Not quite. The Cluny must have done something pretty rotten for you to turn him into an epithet. Exactly what was it?"

Lindy tensed, as if that would protect her from Nick's questions. "I don't like talking about it. There's no point."

"Come on, Professor. Out with it. What did he do to you?" Nick's voice was gentle.

"I never talk about it!" she flared. "So why on earth should I tell *you?* Just to satisfy your curiosity?"

He seemed to consider this for a long moment. "Sooner or later you ought to tell somebody," he said at last. "Or whatever happened will go on festering inside you. And I'm good at keeping a confidence. The best, in fact."

Lindy blew out her breath in exasperation. But there was something about Nick, something in his easy, relaxed manner that made her actually want to confide in him. It didn't make any sense, yet she found herself beginning to talk.

"If you have to know, the Clun—I mean, Donald Cluny and I went to college together. After that we worked for a while at the same firm. But then a wonderful position opened up at a really good university. It was a chance to teach and do research.... Oh, we

both wanted that job." Her words stopped abruptly,
like a flow of lava freezing even as it surged down a
mountainside. But Nick went on looking at her as if
he was truly interested in her story. And soon the
words came again. She couldn't stop them, had to get
them out in a hurry as if, indeed, they had been festering inside her.

"The Cluny betrayed me," she said bitterly. "That's
all there was to it. He didn't care how he got the job,
even if it meant destroying all trust between us. And
he was clever about sabotaging me. Hinted around
that I was only making it as an engineer because our
firm needed its quota of women. He got that job. We
broke up."

"That's too bad. But you're right. Sounds like
you're better off without him." Nick was gazing at her
hand. Lindy glanced down and saw that her fingers
were clenched around the piece of quartz, her knuckles white with the force of her grip. She didn't understand why she was holding the rock so tightly. The
pain and the anger were long past! She stuffed the
quartz back into her pocket, then folded her arms
against her chest.

"It wasn't the job that mattered. Or even that
Donald and I wouldn't be married. It was discovering
our entire relationship had been a fraud. That hurt the
most. But I'm over it now. I've put things into perspective."

Nick gave a faint smile. "Basically, your perspective is to write off the entire male gender because of
one lousy guy. Am I right?"

Now Lindy felt even more defensive with Nick. She
leaned toward him. "After what happened with the

Cluny, I started really listening to some of the other men I worked with. I started really hearing the snide little remarks they made about female engineers. And then I got tired of caring what *any* man said or did. What's so bad about that, anyway?''

"Nothing." But Nick seemed to regard her again with an infuriating mixture of amusement and pity. It had been a mistake for Lindy to tell him any of this. She was a happy person, content with her career and her life. For crying out loud, she didn't need Nick Jarrett's sympathy!

"Jarrett, those owls are in grave danger. That's what I want to talk about. Nothing else."

He gazed at Lindy thoughtfully for another moment, but surprised her by dropping the subject of her misadventures with men. He thumbed through the rest of the folder.

"You sure wrote a lot of letters. Belligerent ones, too."

Lindy straightened. "I'm going to keep on fighting until you change the location of your airplane factory. My owls are going to be safe." She spoke with utter conviction. Nothing would make her give up this battle.

Nick Jarrett tossed the file back into his briefcase. "Listen, Professor. I don't have anything against you personally. You're right about one thing, too. Juliet had no business poking into your private life. Sometimes she goes overboard. I ought to know that better than anyone." His tone was wry. "But this is the way it is. A lot of time and money are already invested in this project—"

"You don't give a hoot about owls, do you?"

He didn't answer at first, seeming to consider her words with utmost seriousness even though his mouth gave a suspicious twitch. "I think it's the owls that are supposed to hoot," he said gravely. "But I happen to like birds. Anything that flies is all right with me."

"Then at least you should be willing to talk about relocating the factory. There are other places around Santiago that would make good building sites, you know."

He shut the briefcase and propped his elbows on it. "Why can't you just move the confounded birds? Heck, I've changed apartments plenty of times. It's kind of fun, getting new neighbors and all." Nick was obviously attempting jocularity, but Lindy could only be serious when it came to the owls.

"Even if some of the birds could be captured and relocated, most of them would hide underground. And it would be impossible to excavate down in those tunnels. Your bulldozers would bury the owls alive!"

"I don't want that to happen any more than you do. But face it, Professor. No matter where I build the factory, some type of wildlife is going to be threatened."

Lindy nodded. "I know there aren't any simple answers. I can't save every creature from harm, but I can help this one colony of owls. If I don't do anything else, at least I can do that." She leaned toward him intently. "I know burrowing owls are common, ordinary birds to most people. Nobody's decided they're endangered yet, so they don't get a lot of attention, like whooping cranes or bald eagles. But their homes are being threatened all over the country. And these little owls matter to *me*. They're my own personal responsibility. Don't you understand?''

He looked beleaguered. "Believe me, I'd like to leave you and your owls to flap around in peace. Do you think I actually wanted to be in charge of this project, out here in the boondocks? I turned it down at first. Had my own plans. But after what I did to Juliet that night, hell, I had to make amends somehow. She thinks building this factory in the middle of nowhere is the best damn idea in the world. So I agreed we'd go ahead with it. It was the least I could do after... after the, uh, incident.''

"I don't understand. What did you do that was so awful? Embezzle company funds?''

"It was worse than that. A lot worse," he said gloomily. He stood and went to look out the window. With a lugubrious expression he watched Hammersmith's head bounce up and down, up and down.

"Did you leak company secrets? Is that it?''

"Worse. Much worse.''

Lindy tried telling herself Nick Jarrett's problems were no concern of hers. But it didn't help. She was still itching with curiosity. "Well, what *did* you do?''

"I owe it to Juliet not to say any more. Heck, we've worked together a long time...." His voice trailed off. He seemed abstracted, lost in his own thoughts. Yet after a moment he went on, "Juliet built up Aldridge Aviation from scratch. And when she wanted to expand the company, I came in as her partner. She knows airplanes almost better than I do. You should see her fly that ancient trimotor of hers. She can roll out of a turn without even one shimmy of her tail. If you think that's easy, try taking the controls of one of those old planes."

A sharp stab of jealousy pierced Lindy. It was completely unexpected, and so disconcerting that she had to stand up. What was happening to her? How could she be jealous of someone like Juliet Aldridge? After all, the woman had sent spies to follow Lindy to the army-surplus store and the frozen-yogurt shop! That hardly made her a commendable person.

But Lindy felt envy, nonetheless, outright envy after hearing the admiration in Nick's voice. Lindy herself hated flying in airplanes of any kind. She much preferred to stay anchored to the solid earth. It was enough to see her owls take wing. But Nick Jarrett wouldn't admire that. He wouldn't be dazzled.

"Oh, for goodness' sake!" she exclaimed. "Enough, already!"

Nick glanced at her. "That's what I say. Enough, already. I have a job to do—build a factory. That's what I'm going to do." He stuffed his hands into the pockets of his rumpled pants, looking stubborn and unyielding. He also looked attractive. The sunlight streaming through the window picked out the gold strands in his tousled hair. His masculinity overwhelmed the small kitchen. He wasn't suited to this cramped space; surely he belonged outdoors, in the open and the wild.

Lindy swung her purse strap over one shoulder. The purse was so heavy she almost listed sideways. But she stood firm and straight as she faced Nick Jarrett. "You still have a chance to negotiate with me about the location of your factory. Before it's too late—before I take the next step."

"What are you going to do? Start throwing rocks at me? Come on, Professor, you're the one who needs to be reasonable. I'm sorry about your owls. Damn sorry. But there's nothing I can do."

Perhaps his regret was sincere. Lindy would allow him that much. But he was still the enemy, and he was refusing to compromise. She angled the brim of her cap. "This is only the beginning, Jarrett. You're in for a long, hard fight with me. And in the end I'm going to win. Because I'm the one who's right."

He smiled faintly. "I get it. This is the good guys against the bad guys. Justice versus injustice. The rhubarb-jam crowd as opposed to the coffee drinkers."

"You can turn it into a joke all you want. But it's not a joke. Not when innocent creatures are threatened just because you're out to make a buck."

He frowned, all lighthearted humor gone. "Look, I build airplanes because . . . because I love airplanes, dammit. Money doesn't have anything to do with it. But it's taken a lot of work to make Aldridge Aviation a success. I'm not going to sacrifice that."

Lindy gazed at him. Before today, her battle had been with Aldridge Aviation, a big impersonal company. Now that she'd met Nick, her enemy had become one man—a man with gold-brown hair and blue eyes who was grouchy in the morning and who promised to be as stubborn as Lindy was herself. He was a dangerous person, a threat to the owls. And he was dangerous in another way, too. Already he seemed to have touched something vulnerable inside her. Being with him reminded her of how she'd felt the last time she'd made the mistake of flying in an airplane. Off balance, out of control...

Lindy shifted her purse onto her other shoulder. She couldn't afford to let him affect her like this. Too much was at stake. "Jarrett, you're going to find something out about me, something that's not in that file Juliet Aldridge gave you. Her spies forgot to report that I'm a very loyal person. I've promised those owls I'll protect them. Nothing—no one—can make me forsake that promise. You haven't seen or heard the last of me!" She turned and marched down the hallway of the trailer. Then she yanked open the front door and took the steps at a clatter, hardly paying attention when Hammersmith greeted her with several joyful slurps of his tongue.

Nick Jarrett had a fight on his hands. But so did Lindy. And she would have to be stronger than ever before. For the owls' sake—and for her own.

LINDY PUNCHED DOWN on the accelerator and shot her little blue car into the self-serve gas station with the expertise of a rally driver. She always drove her best when she was in a desperate hurry. Tonight she simply couldn't afford to be late. Almost a week had passed since her confrontation with Jarrett, but now she had a real chance to fight him. Screeching to a halt next to the one available pump, she scrambled out of her car. A truck pulled up across from her, the driver swinging down from his seat. Nick Jarrett, no less.

She frowned at him. "What are you doing here?" she asked suspiciously.

He frowned back. "I'm on my way to that damn fool meeting of yours—what do you think? But I'm surprised you didn't bring the blond wonder dog with you to cause more havoc.''

"Hammersmith's at home, behaving himself quite well." Lindy didn't mention that whenever she started to go anywhere, Hammers had developed the habit of wrapping both his front legs around her ankles and hanging on for dear life. This evening she'd finally managed to distract him by tossing an apple into the living room. While he chased it she'd sprinted out of the house.

Now Jarrett moved toward the gas pump. Lindy claimed the nozzle before he could get to it.

"I was here first," she asserted. "And I'm not going to be late for the town council meeting because of you."

"Why did you have to drag the whole town into your crusade, anyway? It won't do you any good, and it's only wasting my time." He went over to the gas-station attendant, flipped some money out of his wallet, then came back to his truck. "The next gas is mine. Hand over the pump."

"I told you, I was here first."

"I already paid. So let's just get on with this." Deftly he reached across, took the nozzle and transferred it to his own tank.

Lindy pushed back a strand of her dark hair. The hot summer breeze immediately whipped another strand into her face, as if to taunt her. But she was not defeated. Before Nick could start pumping gas, she seized the nozzle and ferried it back to her own car.

"I was here first, you know. I pulled up at least a second before you did."

"Don't you know anything about the real world?" he complained. "Professor, this is how it is. You pay, you get to pump your gas. Everybody else waits in line."

"Oh, no. That's not how we do it here in Santiago. We believe in a few rules of common courtesy. You get to a pump first, you get to use it first. Doesn't matter who's paid what." Unfortunately, she'd slackened her grip on the handle of the nozzle. Nick easily grabbed it away from her again and started pumping his own gas.

"I have enough problems without being plagued by a crazed rock hound," he muttered. "Let's get this damn council thing out of the way and be done with it."

"You're cranky in the evening, too, not just in the morning. That's a bad sign. You could use a dose of my rhubarb compote, you really could." She tried to reach around him and snatch back the gas nozzle, but he blocked her way.

"Tell you what I could use, Professor Mac. A lot less aggravation from *you*. I've only been here a few days, but you keep popping up in my life like some berserk jack-in-the-box. You're even worse than that dog of yours when he's practicing basketball." He looked her over, his hand still firmly on the nozzle. "You really dressed up for this meeting, didn't you, Eloise? But I miss your baseball hat."

She flushed. She couldn't deny she'd taken a great deal of effort with her appearance. She'd even hauled out a silk blouse from the back of her closet—the blouse Aunt Eloise had given her last Christmas and which she'd never worn. Aunt Eloise was so thrilled to have a namesake that she was always sending Lindy expensive and completely unsuitable gifts. Lindy hated this particular blouse; it had floppy sleeves that kept dangling at her wrists and was a rather alarming shade of purple. But it was the most elegant item of clothing she owned, and tonight it had seemed important to be elegant...feminine. Was that because she wanted to present the best image possible when she addressed the town council—or because she wanted to be attractive for Nick Jarrett?

Lindy flushed more deeply, realizing how foolish she'd been. She'd decked herself out in this uncomfortable blouse, along with a narrow skirt that meant she could take only short, hobbled steps, and hose that made her legs itch. Worst of all were the high-heeled sandals. She glanced down and saw that her feet looked ridiculous stuffed into flimsy shoes like these. Her attempts at feminine frippery hadn't done a bit of good—Nick Jarrett didn't seem at all impressed.

Lindy pulled up her sleeves, trying to anchor them above her elbows. "Jarrett, maybe you think you can get the better of me any time you want. But you're wrong. And you're not going to hurt those owls—"

"Save it for your soapbox at the meeting, Professor Mac." He finished pumping gas and climbed into his truck. Then he leaned out the window. "Let me give you some advice. Go back to your rock hounding and stop harassing law-abiding citizens like me. I'm going to start building right on schedule. There's nothing you can do to prevent that." He stared at her hard, as if to emphasize his words. A moment later his truck wheeled out of the gas station.

"Wait. You can't leave. Come back here!" Lindy yanked up her blasted sleeves again. Nick Jarrett was *not* going to get the better of her. And he certainly wasn't going to arrive at that town council meeting before she did. Fingers crossed that her gas would hold out, Lindy scrambled into her car and sped after him. She could see his truck farther up the road, his broad-shouldered frame clearly visible through the rear window. She floored the gas pedal, gaining on Nick until she was right on his bumper. Tailgating shamelessly, she was close enough to see his eyes narrow as he glanced into his rearview mirror. He accelerated and began surging away.

"No, you don't." She pushed her little car as fast as it would go. It was more than twenty years old, but it was valiant and gave her everything it had. Lindy pulled into the left lane and went rocketing past Nick's truck. She waved triumphantly as she left him behind.

"Yippee! You did it, Sally," she congratulated her car. "You showed him, all right."

Ka-chug, the car stuttered in response. *Ka-chug, Ka-chug . . .*

Lindy didn't like that sound at all. And she didn't like the fact that the needle on the gas gauge had dipped well below empty. The engine was probably running on fumes. "Don't give out on me now, Sally," she pleaded, even though she knew it wasn't any use. Lindy swerved over to the side of the road just as the engine gave one last heave and died.

Lindy groaned in unison with her car. This was awful. Awful and humiliating. It didn't help to have Nick Jarrett park his truck behind her and then come strolling up to her window. He bent down to peer at her.

"Car trouble?" he asked, a false note of concern in his voice.

"It's nothing you need to bother about." She stared straight ahead to avoid gazing into the startling blue of his eyes.

"Well, I'm not sure about that. You seem in a mighty big hurry to get to the meeting, and it wouldn't be gallant of me to leave you stranded here. Why don't I look under the hood to see what's wrong?" He grinned at her. She let out an explosive sigh.

"I'm sure you already know I ran out of gas, pure and simple."

"Say, that's rotten luck. Especially since you were just at a gas station. Doesn't really seem fair, does it?"

He was enjoying himself far too much. He propped his hand on the roof of her car, leaning a bit closer. Lindy caught a whiff of his scent—brisk and tangy. For some reason it reminded her of chocolates, the ones with mint centers that were always such a delightful surprise when she bit into them. Her mouth began to water.

Goodness, what was happening to her? Swinging open her door, she made Nick hop out of the way. She dragged her purse along with her as she stood up and gave Nick a cool perusal.

"You actually think you have all the power, don't you, Jarrett? You think I'm just a college teacher and no real danger to your almighty Aldridge Aviation. But you're making a mistake. You shouldn't underestimate me."

He shrugged. "You want to talk power, Professor Mac, we'll talk power. This is how I see it—each of us has a vehicle, but mine's the only one that can go anywhere. So I guess I do have the upper hand, at least for now."

Lindy glanced along this sleepy country lane. A few adobe houses were sprawled here and there among beds of irises and hollyhocks. Mellow evening sunlight deepened the green and dark purple of the alfalfa fields; a breeze rustled the leaves of the cottonwood trees. It was a peaceful scene—too peaceful by far. The lushness of this Rio Grande valley surrounded Lindy and Nick in their own private world. No other cars were in sight. Only a roadrunner darted across the asphalt, spreading his wings to skim an irrigation ditch. His long tail bobbed in the air, and then even he was gone. Lindy was stranded here—stranded alone with Nick Jarrett.

CHAPTER THREE

"OKAY, OKAY. You'll have to give me a ride to the meeting. Let's get going. If we hurry, we won't be that late." Lindy spoke forcefully, but Nick behaved as if they had hours to spare. He walked all the way around her car, examining its various nicks and scars.

"Not really in bad shape," he said, running a hand along Sally's one remaining strip of silver trim. "Original paint job, too. Not bad, not bad at all for an antique. And look at the lines of this thing, streamlined enough to fly. Go ahead, take a really good look at your car. Doesn't it remind you of a Sopwith Camel minus the wings?"

Lindy drew her eyebrows together. Her faithful old car did, indeed, have curving lines that might well have been suited to an airplane. It wasn't difficult at all to imagine Sally sprouting wings and chugging off into the skies.

But Nick wasn't yet finished examining her car. He squinted, trying to gain a better view through one of the dusty windows.

"You have rocks in there, too," he said in disbelief. "Big rocks. Lord, that one's a boulder. How'd you cram it through the door? Amazing, that's all I can say. No wonder you ran out of gas. You're so weighted down you must get the worst mileage this side of the Mississippi.''

Lindy swiped her hand over some of the grime on Sally's windows. ''Those are all important specimens, every one of them. Are we going to the meeting, or what?''

''I like the sound of 'or what,''' Nick remarked. But at last he headed toward the truck.

Lindy gave her car one last pat. ''I'm sorry, Sally, but I have to leave you here,'' she murmured. ''I'll come back later, don't worry.''

Nick glanced at her. ''Sally?'' he echoed. ''So you're one of those people who name inanimate objects, like cars and toasters. Interesting.''

''I've never named a toaster in my life.'' She bit her lip, wishing she hadn't let Sally's name slip out. It was a very personal, private name, so private that not even Juliet Aldridge's spies had found out about it. But here Lindy was, blabbing her secret in front of Nick. He affected her in so many contrary ways. ''Haven't you ever given an airplane some nickname you didn't want anyone else to know? Answer me that.''

He looked disgruntled, and she knew she'd struck a nerve. Undoubtedly there was an airplane somewhere with a silly name dreamed up by Nick. Unfortunately this made him all the more appealing to her. Blast it! She had to stop being attracted to the man. Right now, she had to stop!

Lindy marched over to his truck and climbed into the passenger seat. She rested her purse in her lap, reassured by its good, solid weight. She was tempted to reach inside and fish out a chunk of quartz; nothing was more soothing to her than rubbing her fingers over quartz. But she didn't care to have Nick make any more jokes about her fondness for rocks. She kept her hands clasped together on top of her purse, waiting as he climbed into the driver's seat. Now they could be on their way.

But Nick didn't start the engine. Instead he turned toward her, leaning back against the door and balancing one arm on the steering wheel. He studied her with a solemn expression.

Lindy shifted position, her skirt catching on the nubby upholstery. She'd worn this skirt so few times the material was still new and stiff; she felt as if she'd wrapped herself in a piece of cardboard. "Can we go?" she asked.

"Look at it like this. They can't start the meeting without you and me there. So what's our hurry?"

"I know what you're trying to do. You're trying to delay so we don't get to the meeting at all. But you can forget your underhanded tactics! I'll walk all the way there, if that's what it takes." She reached for the door handle.

"Hold on. I'll get both of us to your confounded meeting. But first I'm going to ask you a few questions."

Lindy didn't like Nick's types of questions. She was all set to jump out of the truck and go jogging down the road. But she knew she wouldn't make very good time in this skirt and these absurd sandals. And Nick was already asking away.

"How the heck did you end up with a name like Linden Eloise?"

She plucked at her sleeves. Maybe it was her imagination, but this darn blouse seemed to be growing more billowy and unmanageable by the minute. "I'm sure your spy report can tell you whatever you need to know about me. I want to talk about how you're going to pick a new location to build your airplane factory."

"Linden . . . Isn't that a tree, or something?"

"Oh, good grief. I was named for my father. I'm Linden Jr. I would've been named for my mother, too, only 'Linden Agatha' was a little much—even in my parents' opinion. Aunt Eloise came to help out when I was born, and one thing led to another. Just my luck that Aunt Alayne couldn't make it for a visit—her name I could have lived with. Anyway, except for my students, everyone calls me Lindy. There. That's the whole story. Satisfied?"

He chuckled. "Lindy. It suits you. Did you know that was Charles Lindbergh's nickname? Now, there was a pilot for you." He stared out the windshield, as if hoping the *Spirit of St. Louis* would materialize from the clouds and go soaring above him.

It was Lindy's turn to be curious. "You really do love airplanes and flying and all that, don't you?"

"Hey, from the time I was five years old I knew I was going to fly planes some day. I never wanted to do anything else. Lindy, the grandest feeling I know is to be up there alone in a single-seater, practically nothing between me and the sky. Big planes aren't for me. Forget your jet engines, your turbines. Give me cylinders and propellers any day." He gestured so exuberantly that one of his hands smacked against the steering wheel, but he didn't seem to notice. The evening sun picked out the gold strands in his hair until it was easy to imagine his enthusiasm had sparked a fire on top of his head. He was so vibrant. In spite of Lindy's better judgment, she wanted to know more about him. And she wanted to know about the things that made him wave his arms in such excitement.

"Building airplanes—that can't be nearly as much fun as flying them. Do you really have the career you want at Aldridge Aviation?" She was hoping he'd answer that Aldridge wasn't actually his cup of tea—or cup of coffee, to be more accurate. But, if anything, Nick grew more enthusiastic.

"In this business, every stage of the game is fascinating. Design, construction, test flight. Best time I ever had was designing the Aldridge Sparrow a couple of years ago. Three hours of sleep a night, that's all I was getting back then."

"Heavens, you must have been grouchier than ever."

"Heck, no. I hardly needed to sleep. Couldn't wait to be at the drafting board every morning. And I'm going to make sure I have another chance at that. Once this Santiago project is under way, I'm going to get back into design." His hand thumped against the steering wheel again, this time hitting the horn. A loud honk punctuated his words like an exclamation point.

"I guess you and Juliet Aldridge make a pretty good team." Lindy hated herself for what she was doing now—fishing to learn more about the relationship between Nick and Juliet. But she couldn't seem to stop herself. "I mean, the two of you are both involved with airplanes. You share something."

Nick didn't answer. An expression came over his face that Lindy couldn't quite describe. It did, however, remind her of the way her own face had puckered up that time she'd tried eating two sour grapefruits in a row for breakfast.

"Yeah, well, Juliet does believe in sharing," he said at last, his voice tinged with irony. "At least, when a person's on her good side. And I'm definitely not on her good side. I probably won't be for the next century or so."

"What exactly did you do to her?"

"Let's just say that, according to Juliet, I've committed the worst sin since Adam and Eve ate that apple."

"Yes, but what sin?"

"Look, I've already told you too much. I promised Juliet I'd keep the story quiet. I guess she deserves that much from me."

Lindy couldn't resist any longer. She dug into her purse and randomly grabbed a piece of gypsum. It wasn't as suitable as quartz for soothing the emotions, perhaps; gypsum was a bit too uneven in texture. But it still might be an antidote for the annoying interest Lindy was developing in Nick. She curled her fingers over the rock. Goodness, what *had* happened between him and Juliet Aldridge?

He settled back comfortably in his seat. "Seems to me we were discussing you, Professor Mac. Here's what I want to know. Don't you ever get lonely in this little town in the middle of nowhere? Especially with no boyfriend." He was teasing her again, humor playing over his face. Lindy wished she could think of something flippant and witty as a retort. But nothing came to mind. For some reason, she couldn't think very clearly when she was gazing into Nick's eyes.

"I have my classes to teach. I don't really have time to get lonely, not with so many students." Lindy smiled, remembering her students of the past few years. They came in all ages, all types—some fresh out of high school, some on retirement, others struggling to hold down jobs, raise families and still find time for school. Each person Lindy taught gave something special to her in return, something unique. Altogether, her students provided her with an incredible amount of emotional fulfillment. What else could she wish for?

As Lindy smiled to herself, the dusky air throbbed with the call of a single, lonely bird. The summer breeze stirred through the open windows of the truck, playing with her hair. And Nick reached over to caress her cheek, his touch as gentle and tantalizing as the warm breeze.

"What are you doing?" Lindy's voice had suddenly developed an odd shakiness.

"I think that's fairly obvious. I'm getting ready to kiss you."

"Why?" was all she could ask.

"I don't know. Maybe it's just the way you looked a minute ago—so privately happy. Do you have a good reason why I shouldn't kiss you?"

"No," she whispered, her heart pounding as if she'd sprinted up a mountain. The stick shift was proving a serious impediment to Nick as he maneuvered closer to her. Lindy did some maneuvering of her own, colliding awkwardly with Nick in the center of the bench seat. The heavy purse in her lap was another obstacle as she and Nick bumped against each other. But he managed to put his hands on her shoulders, bend his head and place his mouth firmly on hers.

The piece of gypsum fell from Lindy's grasp and dropped onto the floorboard. Her eyelids drifted downward, and somehow one of her feet slipped from the confines of its sandal. Oh, what a kiss—thorough, decisive, immensely satisfying. It had a beginning, a middle and an end, like a well-told story. The beginning was an exquisite lesson in every contour of Nick's mouth. The middle was simple enjoyment of his taste and touch and minty scent. And the end of the kiss found Lindy leaning breathlessly against him, her fingers twined in his shaggy hair.

It took her at least a full minute to sit upright, find her sandal and yank up her sleeves. She peered around for her piece of gypsum, but it seemed to have rolled under the seat.

Nick grinned. "Well, I found out one thing, Professor. You're soft. Just about as soft and warm as a woman can be. You're not at all tough, the way you like to pretend."

Lindy touched her lips with the tips of her fingers, as if she could trace the imprint Nick's mouth had left on hers. "I don't have to pretend anything," she murmured distractedly. "I've become very self-sufficient, that's the truth of it. I don't need to be swept away by any kisses...." Oh, darn, she sounded like her brain had turned into cotton candy. That was the effect Nick Jarrett had on her.

He gave a low chuckle that sent ripples of warmth right down to her toes. The sun had dipped low and was no longer shining on his head. His hair looked more brown than gold now, but still much too attractive. Lindy remembered how his hair had felt under her fingers. Surprisingly silky. She longed to run her hands through it some more.

She made a supreme effort to turn her head and gaze straight out the windshield. "Are you ever going to drive me to that meeting?"

Nick chuckled again. "Whatever you say, Professor. Here we go." He started the engine, then revved it. The truck surged onto the road with a power that sent Lindy bouncing back against her seat. She wished she could say something to put that kiss of Nick's in its proper place. Instead, the memory of the kiss lingered, tantalizing her like an unseen feather brushing gently against her mouth. Lindy delved into her purse, found some lip gloss and applied it with resolve. But even that didn't seem to erase the darn kiss!

She was relieved when a short while later Nick pulled into the parking lot of Chamberlin Tech—her beloved institute of technology. She'd arranged for the meeting to be held here, convincing the town councillors that only a large lecture hall could accommodate the crowd expected to show up. But she'd had a much more personal reason in mind, also. This was her territory, the place where she belonged. When she wasn't out roaming the mesa or exploring the mountains, she wanted to be right here at the college. This was where she could share her joy in nature. One of her great satisfactions in life was seeing her students discover the hidden wonder in a cross-bedding of rock or the unexpected beauty in a swirl of ropy lava.

Now Lindy slid down from Nick's truck. The grounds of the college were beautiful, with tree-shaded lawns and beds of riotous petunias. She glanced over at Nick to see if he was appreciating the white stucco buildings with their gracefully arched windows and roofs of red tile; surely nowhere else could he find such charming architecture. But he wasn't paying attention to his surroundings at all. He'd propped his briefcase on the hood of the truck and was rooting through it, grumbling under his breath about "this puny pit stop of a town." He finally found what he was looking for—an elegant paisley tie—and proceeded to flip it under the collar of his shirt, knotting it with rapid expertise. Lindy was impressed as she watched him. He'd take first prize at any tie-tying contest, she was sure of that. He rolled down his sleeves, buttoned his cuffs, straightened his collar...and there he was, the picture of a powerful business executive. Yet a few minor details marred his image. His shirt bore two creases down the front, as if he hadn't unfolded it from his suitcase until today. He was wearing well-tailored trousers, but they were rumpled as if he'd slept in them a few nights. And she could tell he wasn't used to having his hair this long; he tried to shove it away from his forehead and then frowned when a shock of hair flopped down again. Lindy suppressed a smile. It was difficult, for the smile threatened to spread itself across her entire face. But she didn't want to react to Nick Jarrett like this—feeling light and happy just to be standing here, looking at him.

"You know something?" she said. "It really annoys me how you're always saying Santiago is a dinky little town out in the middle of nowhere. Because that's not the way it is at all. Santiago has everything. Art and theater and music and mountains. So you can stop making all your comments about us. Look around and see what's really here. Why, right over there, for instance. See that robin? You're not going to find a better robin anywhere, I can promise you that.''

Nick peered in the direction she pointed out. ''Well, I'll grant you, that is one fat robin. Never seen one that huge. What do you feed them out here—cake and ice cream?''

''It's plump, that's all,'' Lindy countered. ''Robins are supposed to be plump.'' Nonetheless, she was glad to see the bird waddle away over the grass, disappearing behind a tree.

''Okay, so you grow obese robins in Santiago. I'm supposed to be impressed?''

Lindy faced him, her chin tilted so she could look straight into his eyes. ''Tell me one thing about St. Louis, Missouri, that's any better than what we have here in Santiago. Just one thing.''

''Maybe our robins aren't as hefty as yours, but we do have the Cardinals for the best baseball in the world. Heck, we have the Mississippi River, the Gateway Arch and—''

''I hate big cities,'' Lindy declared, hoping to shut him up.

''I hate dinky little towns in the middle of nowhere.''

They scowled at each other. Then Lindy began marching along the sidewalk. Usually her stride was brisk and sure, but tonight she'd taken only a few steps before she stumbled in her cramped shoes. Nick caught up to her and grabbed her elbow. She tried to shake him off.

"Will you let go of me? I can manage on my own."

"Apparently you can't. First you run out of gas, and now you almost fall flat on your face. Good thing you have a man around, isn't it?" He held on to her and propelled her along the sidewalk, his briefcase swinging easily from his other hand. Lindy's heavy, rock-filled purse bumped against her hip—thump, thump, thump. It was a familiar rhythm, one that, over the years, had created worn spots on most of her clothes. Well, there was no chance of that happening with *this* skirt. After tonight she'd toss it back in the closet and never again try to impress Nick Jarrett!

"Wait a minute," she protested. "The meeting's that way."

He changed tack, swiveling her around with him. "Fine, fine. Let's just get on with it. I'm ready."

"Not half as ready as I am."

"I'm more than ready," he muttered.

"You haven't even seen ready yet."

"Do you ever do anything but argue, Professor?"

"I'm not an argumentative person. Not in the least. You're the one causing trouble here."

Nick gave her a sardonic glance. At last they entered the building where the meeting was to take place. Lindy stopped outside the closed door of the lecture hall and pried Nick's fingers from her elbow.

"We're going in there separately. It won't look good for me to sashay in with you in front of the town council."

Nick leaned against the wall, a slow grin coming over his face. "Well, now, Professor Mac. I never suspected you were the type of person to worry about propriety." He took hold of her elbow again, this time with a caressing touch. Lindy backed away, but not before a shiver of delight ran through her. She rubbed her elbow vigorously.

"You know what I mean. You and I—we're on opposite sides of the fence. Let's not give anyone the false impression that we're pleased with each other."

The light shining down from a bulb overhead caught the glint of humor in Nick's eyes. "You mean I don't get to consort with the enemy? I'm disappointed. Very disappointed."

He was teasing her—making fun of her. She knew that, and she knew that she ought to make a withering comment in return. Instead all she could do was gaze at him. Even the dim light from one electric bulb could turn Nick's hair to deep, burnished gold. It was a brown-gold as rich in color as the gleaming wood floors and paneling in this old building. Lindy raised her hand, her fingers quite prepared to run themselves through Nick's hair. It was texture as well as color that enticed her. Nick's hair possessed a silkiness she'd only begun to explore. . . .

Lindy controlled her wayward hand, forcing it to scratch her own ear instead of reaching out to Nick. "Jarrett, I've had enough fribbling from you," she said, only to find him laughing at her again.

"I've only begun to fribble, Professor Mac. In my book, a person can never do too much fribbling."

Oh, for Pete's sake! Here she was, lingering in a classroom hallway like one of her sillier students, exchanging nonsense with an outrageously attractive man. Before the situation could get any worse, Lindy pulled open the door and hurried into the lecture hall. Then she stopped in dismay.

CHAPTER FOUR

LINDY CAME to such a sudden halt that Nick collided with her from behind. He put his hand on her shoulder to steady her, and the two of them ended up looking like the best of friends, after all. Not that it mattered much. There were only three people in the room. One, two, three. That was it. Two town councillors lounging in desks at the front and one of Lindy's students sitting by himself at the very back.

"Did everyone else leave?" she asked, struggling with her disappointment.

One of the councillors, Oliver Caldwell, stood up and stretched. It was a complicated stretch, involving several rotations of his arms and a cracking of knuckles at the end. Lindy winced.

"No one has left," Oliver said in his careful, concise way. He folded his bony hands over his stomach and studied a point somewhere off in the distance.

"You mean . . . no one else showed up?" Lindy asked, her dismay growing.

"That is correct." Oliver's fingers twitched, as if he was getting ready to crack his knuckles again.

"But all the fliers I distributed. The doors I knocked on, the phone calls I made . . ." Lindy's voice trailed off as she glanced around the lecture hall. It seemed cavernous with so few people, like a giant box with five little jelly beans rattling around inside. Lindy cleared her throat and tried to recover some of her usual classroom forcefulness.

"What about the other councillors?" she demanded. "Why aren't they here?"

Oliver cracked his knuckles in reply, making Lindy jump. Melanie Deams spoke up.

"Oliver and I are representing the town council, Lindy. You can't blame the others for not coming. After all, this isn't any official meeting, is it? And nobody wanted to miss the big tournament tonight over at Stop'n'Bowl. What kind of turnout did you expect, anyway?"

"I expected at least a little interest in wildlife preservation," Lindy retorted. But Melanie didn't seem to notice her caustic tone. The woman was giving Nick a big smile and flexing her feet for his benefit. Melanie had pretty, slender feet and good legs to go with them. Nick seemed to be appreciating Melanie's flexing abilities. Stupendous. Lindy hoped he and Melanie's feet would be very happy together. But she had more important things to think about. She disengaged herself from Nick and went to the table at the front of the room. Heaving her purse onto it, she surveyed her meager audience.

In the very back row was Eric Sotelo, one of Lindy's best students. Eric never talked in class, but he performed brilliantly on exams. Tonight he'd ducked behind his notebook the minute Lindy had entered the lecture hall. She knew by now that he wished fervently to be ignored in any public gathering. Little by little she'd been trying to draw him out, but she wasn't going to push it. So she merely nodded at him—or rather, at the notebook he was holding up as protection.

Meanwhile, Oliver Caldwell sat down again, arranging his long limbs with difficulty. He ended up spreading himself over at least two desks, looking like an octopus that didn't know where to drape its tentacles. Nick took a seat a few desks away from Melanie, who casually clasped her hands behind her head. This pose demonstrated that her feet were not the only shapely part of her anatomy. She flashed another smile at Nick. Nick smiled back. Lindy wanted to knock their heads together.

Well, there was nothing to do but plunge straight into this debate. Two or three people were just as important as a whole crowd. If Lindy could sway Oliver, Melanie and Eric over to the owls' side, that would be a great accomplishment. She took a piece of chalk and wrote one word on the blackboard in large, bold letters: POISON. Eric lowered his notebook a bit and even Melanie stopped looking at Nick for a moment.

"Poison," Lindy stated. "Poison in insecticides has already threatened the North American burrowing owl. Picture yourselves on a diet of beetles, grasshoppers, mice—every precious morsel contaminated. Keep picturing yourselves as a colony of owls fighting for survival. There are so many threats. Terrain you once roamed has been converted to farmlands or housing developments or shopping malls. You've been driven out, torn from your homes. Where do you go? Perhaps you'll be lucky enough to find some corner of land that's been deserted by other owls. But there's something you don't know. Airplanes have flown over this land, spraying it with insecticides. That's why no other birds are here. That's why you, too, will eventually die from the poison. You're caught in a tragic cycle of struggle and death.''

She paused, allowing her words to settle in the room. She had everyone's complete attention. Nick was frowning, his eyebrows drawn together. Melanie was nibbling on a fingernail and gazing expectantly at Lindy. Oliver hadn't cracked his knuckles once while she'd been speaking. Eric sat with his chin in his hand, watching her with a dreamy expression.

Lindy allowed this pause to stretch out; she was creating a deliberate tension in the room. She'd learned long ago that successful teaching involved a healthy dose of showmanship. And right now she was more a teacher than ever before, trying everything she knew to stir up her audience.

After another moment she went on, ''Suppose that you—a small burrowing owl—have found at last one patch of earth where you can survive. The grasshoppers and the mice you feed on haven't yet been contaminated. You're safe—almost. Because now there's a new threat. Aldridge Aviation.'' She stared at Nick. ''Aldridge Aviation is going to bring in its bulldozers, destroy your burrows, kill your young. And maybe after that you won't just be homeless anymore. Maybe you'll actually be extinct.''

Melanie drew in her breath with a little catch. Oliver still refrained from cracking his knuckles. Eric propped his chin in his other hand, never taking his eyes off Lindy. And Nick stood up and came to confront her on the other side of the table. He looked angry.

"Just a minute. I demand equal time after that assault of yours. You've practically accused me of setting out to destroy the entire owl population of the United States. You're being melodramatic, you're using sensationalism, and you're just plain overreacting!"

Lindy folded her arms tightly against her body. "It won't do you any good to attack *me,* Jarrett. What you need to do is defend your own position. Frankly, I don't think you can."

He leaned toward her, propping his hands on the table. "I've already told you about all the time and money Aldridge Aviation has poured into that property. Do you actually expect us to sell it and find another piece of land, just like that?"

"I know it won't be easy or convenient for you. But it's the only solution, no matter how difficult it may be. So, yes—that's precisely what I expect you to do."

"Ha. Even if we did something absurd like sell the land, you'd still raise a ruckus, Linden *Eloise.* You'd complain that we'd sold it to someone who wanted to build a housing development or a supermarket. And your owls wouldn't be any better off than before."

"I believe you've raised an excellent point," she said, her voice cool. "You're right. Before you close any deals, I'll need to know who's buying the land from you."

"We're not going to sell it, Eloise. Got that?"

She leaned toward him from her side of the table until her mouth was almost touching his ear. "Don't call me that name anymore," she whispered fiercely. "You know how much I hate it. You're using unfair tactics, and you still haven't defended your position."

"Who's being unfair here?" Nick muttered back into her ear. "You talk about poison in one breath, and me in the next. You're not even being subtle about it."

"Guys, this isn't a private argument, you know," Melanie complained. She sounded like a kid left out of a hopscotch game on the playground. Lindy's ear was tingling from its close contact with Nick's mouth. She straightened quickly.

"Okay, Melanie. What's your opinion about all this?"

Melanie waited for Nick to look at her, then tossed her head back and forth until her cap of short, silvery blond hair gave a winsome bounce. Lindy stifled a sigh; her own hair was unruly and incapable of even a modest bounce.

"This is the way I see it," Melanie said. "The story you told about owls, Lindy—that was really something. For a minute there I almost *felt* like an owl, and like everybody was after me. And you know, it's not fair."

"You're absolutely right. It's not fair," Lindy affirmed.

Melanie Deams looked sad and thoughtful. Then she shook her head, as if in regret. "I sure don't want to hurt any owls. But having a new factory is going to bring all sorts of jobs to Santiago. It's going to be very good for our economy. I have to tell myself that people are more important than anything else. And I figure if you want to feel sorry for something—what about all those mice that get chomped by owls? None of it's fair. I know this may sound ruthless, but we're the highest up on the food chain. We do what we have to do. And that means we should help Aldridge Aviation every way we can. Let's bring jobs to Santiago!''

Melanie seemed relieved at the course of her own logic, and she smiled again. She possessed an infectious smile, unabashedly wide. No wonder Nick responded to it and smiled right back. But did he have to be quite so responsive? He was grinning from ear to ear.

''I want Santiago to have jobs, too,'' Lindy said. ''That's not the issue. What I'm asking is that Aldridge Aviation consider a more appropriate location.''

Melanie came to stand by Nick. She was petite, the top of her head barely even with his shoulder. She nestled so close to him that she looked like a pretty silver flower twining up a trellis. And Nick didn't seem to mind being the trellis.

''Lindy, if we're not careful, Nick will find a location somewhere far away from Santiago. We can't let that happen. Absolutely not.'' Melanie patted Nick's arm as if to reassure him, and then her expression became serious. ''Our economy is healthy, but we do need to stimulate growth in our labor force. Aldridge Aviation is giving us a perfect opportunity. And we have so much to offer in return! Several nearby market centers, modern transportation routes and strong banking institutions. Not to mention town councillors who are both single *and* friendly.'' Melanie was being cute, perky, smart and witty all at the same time. Lindy didn't know if she could take much more, especially when Nick chuckled and looked down into Melanie's big hazel eyes.

"Oliver, what do you have to say?" Lindy asked, hoping for support. Oliver took a long time to answer. At last he cracked his knuckles.

"Don't have anything against owls," he said. "But jobs are good, can't deny that. Cooperation with Aldridge. That's the ticket."

Lindy almost groaned out loud. How could Oliver be so long on limbs and so short on words? And they were the wrong words. Eric huddling there in the back of the room wasn't being much help, either. He bent over his notebook, scribbling away as if taking notes in one of Lindy's classes.

"I don't think we have anything more to talk about," Melanie said cheerfully. "I'm sure the other councillors would agree with Oliver and me—we're going to do everything in our power to help Aldridge Aviation."

"That's it?" Lindy demanded. "That's all any of you have to say?"

Eric bent lower over his notebook. Oliver pursed his lips and stared off into the distance. Melanie snuggled up to Nick. Lindy surveyed the lot of them and announced, "This is wonderful. Just great. Meeting adjourned!"

Melanie gave all her attention to Nick Jarrett. "Nicky, why don't you join me for a drink tonight? I'd love to start showing you Santiago's attractions."

He looked regretful. "Sorry, but Professor MacAllister and I still have some business together."

"The meeting's over, Nicky."

"I can tell the professor's not finished with me yet."

"Really..." Melanie obviously didn't like being cast aside. She tossed her head, and this time her hair gave a most belligerent bounce. "I suppose I'll have to take a rain check, then. We *will* get together, Nicky." Slowly, reluctantly, she untwined herself from him. She hovered around as if hoping he'd change his mind. Finally she sauntered from the room, giving Nick one last view of her shapely legs.

Oliver undraped his body from several desks and started loping toward the door. "Good meeting," he pronounced to Lindy as he passed her. "Just the way I like 'em. Short and sweet." Then he, too, was gone. Only Eric remained, still scribbling away furiously. After a moment he glanced up, looking alarmed. Grabbing his notebook, he scrambled from his seat and scurried out the door of the lecture hall. And that was the end of Lindy's glorious meeting. What visions she'd had for it! Crowds of townspeople, gathering in support of her and the owls... but here she was, alone in the room with Nick Jarrett. So much for visions. Lindy snatched an eraser and started cleaning the blackboard. Chalk dust flew.

"You know, I didn't agree with most of what you said tonight," Nick told her. "But I have to admit... you were effective. You're good in front of a classroom, Professor. Damn good."

"I guess that's why I have the unwavering support of the town council behind me." Anger and frustration churned inside Lindy, and she fairly scrubbed the blackboard.

"You gave it your best try. You can't ask more from yourself than that. Relax."

Lindy grimaced. Her meeting had been a wretched failure, and he was telling her to relax! Now he took the eraser from her. He wiped the blackboard, the last of POISON disappearing under his broad, even strokes.

"You know, this takes me back," he remarked. "I used to stay after school and clean the board for my fifth-grade teacher, Miss Payton. I had a crush on her the entire year. There's something irresistible about schoolteachers." His tone was light. "That kid who sat in the back seat tonight, he understands what I'm talking about."

Nick's good humor was really grating on Lindy's nerves. Of course, he didn't have anything to be upset about. The meeting had been a resounding success for him; Melanie Deams was going to court him, and apparently so was the rest of the town. Lindy snatched the eraser back. She went at the blackboard again even though Nick had already cleaned it.

"For your information, Eric Sotelo doesn't have a crush on me. He's a very good student and he'll make a fine engineer some day. Naturally he pays attention to his teachers."

"One teacher in particular." Nick took the eraser from her again. "You're doing it all wrong," he said. "You should erase up and down, not side to side. There's a real technique to this sort of thing." He demonstrated wide strokes up and down the blackboard, the strong muscles moving under his shirt.

Blast it, this was *her* classroom and she knew darn well how to clean a blackboard. She wrested the eraser away from him and attacked the board in a defiant side-to-side motion. "You think you can come to

Santiago and take charge of everything, don't you? The whole dinky little town at your command.''

"Hey, I've just been trying to mind my own business since I came here."

"And heaven help a few little owls who get in the way of your business. You're not going to hurt them, Nick. Even if no one else in town will support me, I'll protect them from you."

"Don't get melodramatic again. Nobody's the villain here."

"Fine. Don't take any responsibility. That's an answer." She twisted around toward him. "You don't care how much those owls will suffer. You don't care at all!"

By now his good humor had completely vanished. The lines of his face hardened. "Lindy, you know that's not true. You haven't made even one attempt to see my viewpoint in this."

"I can't find anything valid about your viewpoint."

"So we're back to that again. You're the only one who's right."

"At least I have that much," she declared. "Knowing I *am* right. And that's why I'll win in the end." She turned back toward the blackboard, but Nick grasped her shoulders. She could see the anger darkening his eyes.

"Dammit, somehow I'll make you see there are two sides to this, Lindy."

"Yes, but there's only one side that matters."

His hands tightened on her. "Do you really think you can go through life this rigid and uncompromising?"

She struggled to free herself, her own anger flaring higher. "Some things can't be compromised! Let go of me."

"Not until you see reason. Not until you admit that at least there's room for discussion here."

"You've already tried to justify yourself, and you can't. Let go!"

Instead he pulled her closer. "No wonder you haven't allowed a man into your life," he said in a low, mocking voice. "You only know how to be tender and yielding for creatures who can't threaten you. Those owls are useful to you, aren't they? Because your tenderness has to come out somehow, Professor Mac."

"Damn you, Nick—"

He didn't let her say anything more, his mouth taking harsh possession of hers. She struggled wildly a moment longer, like one of her owls in captivity. She and Nick bumped against the table. But then the eraser dropped from her hand, falling to the floor. She was lost in a heady swirl of chalk dust . . . and she was lost in Nick Jarrett's arms.

CHAPTER FIVE

THIS TIME Nick wasn't gentle—but neither was Lindy. She kissed him with a passion that was still part anger. Her fingers twined behind his neck, and the feel of his hair was as silky and vibrant as she remembered. She strained against him until he was forced to sit abruptly on the table. Once he recovered his balance, his arms tightened around her. His mouth bruised hers with a hunger she returned full measure. This was no schoolgirl's kiss. Oh, no. One touch from Nick, and all of Lindy's long-buried needs began to stir and awaken. She didn't want that! But she allowed herself one more moment of abandoned delight in his arms. One more moment, and then another...

Somehow, at last, she pulled away from him, stumbling back until she was pressed against the blackboard. She reached behind her and randomly grabbed a piece of chalk. She needed something to hold on to, something familiar and reassuring.

Nick remained half seated on the edge of the table, his eyes dark. "What's got you so scared, Lindy? That you might end up feeling a little affection for me instead of despising me wholeheartedly?"

Lindy rolled the piece of chalk between her hands until her palms were white. "I despise what you're doing, not who you are. Maybe you're the nicest man in the world. I don't know. But that doesn't change the fact that you're wrong when it comes to the owls. One hundred percent wrong. Completely, entirely, un-equivocally wrong!"

"Someday maybe you'll learn you can accomplish a lot more by bending a little, giving a little." Nick straightened up from the table and stepped close to Lindy. She pressed so hard against the blackboard it was a wonder her spine didn't simply meld itself into the slate surface.

"What are you trying to do, Jarrett? Kiss me into submission? It hasn't worked yet."

"Lord, you know that's not why I kissed you. There's something between us that doesn't have any-thing at all to do with your confounded owls. And that's what really has you scared."

Lindy couldn't seem to find a retort to that. All she could do was look at Nick's mouth. It was a wide, ex-pressive mouth, generous with any emotion. Gener-ous with humor and equally so with desire...

She tried to focus on a more neutral spot, such as his chin. There was only one problem. His jaw was strongly molded and tantalized her with its shadow of gold beard. Lindy wished Nick wouldn't shave, ever. She suspected he could grow a very decent beard, full and luxuriant....

"This has gone far enough!" she exclaimed, grip-ping her chalk. "Will you *stop*, Jarrett?"

He frowned at her. "Don't worry. I'm not going to kiss you again. Not right this minute, anyway."

Lindy set the chalk on the ledge of the blackboard, wiping her hands decisively on her skirt. Now two white spots adorned the fabric like smudged angel's wings. She heaved her purse strap over one shoulder. Whenever she went too long a time without the comforting bulk of her purse, she began to feel off balance, as if she could maintain true equilibrium only with this heavy weight tugging one way or another.

She marched to the door, turning back for a moment to glance at Nick. "Maybe everything you say about me is true—that I'm rigid and unyielding and narrow-minded. And that I'm scared to feel anything personal for you. Fine. Because those are exactly the qualities I need to fight you and win. Nothing else matters. Now, good night. I'm going home."

Lindy was learning how to travel fast in these wretched shoes. With a combination of jogging and hobbling, she reached the parking lot in record time— only to remember that her little blue car was still stranded on a country lane. Out of gas.

She stood in front of Nick's truck, exasperated. She'd made such a good exit! And now it was ruined. Nick walked toward her under the old-fashioned lampposts that lighted the sidewalk as twilight deepened.

"Need a ride?" he asked in a conversational tone. She glared at him. He opened the passenger door, and without a word she got into the cab of his truck.

Neither one of them spoke on the way back to the gas station. For some reason Lindy was thoroughly annoyed at Nick's having an empty gas can on hand. And he paid for the gas to put into it before she could fumble past all the rocks in her purse to find her wallet. That was even more annoying. She refused to be indebted to him and slapped some dollar bills on the dashboard of his truck. He merely scowled at the money. Then he drove to where her car was parked, swung out of the truck and started dumping the gas into Sally's tank. Lindy hobbled to his side.

"Let me do that," she said, trying to take the can away from him.

"Hey, you're going to spill the gas." He held on to the can.

"You can leave now. Everything's under control." She wouldn't let go of the can, either. And so, pouring gas into Sally's parched tank turned out to be a joint effort. Afterward Nick nudged the can toward her.

"Keep this. You might as well be prepared for future emergencies."

"What happened tonight was an exceptional case. And it was all *your* fault." But somehow Lindy ended up holding the blasted can, with its reek of gas fumes. She knew she ought to push it right back at him. Instead, she cradled it against her silk blouse as if he'd just presented her with a bouquet of roses. What was wrong with her?

Lindy thumped her hand on the can, producing a hollow *thunk*. "Good night, Nick. You really can leave now."

"Good night." He didn't move.

"Would you go, already?"

"I'm not going to leave you out here on a deserted road. Get in and see if your car starts."

"I can take care of myself."

He stayed where he was. Muttering in disgust, Lindy stuffed herself, her purse and her gas can into the car. She started the engine, then poked her head out the window. "Satisfied?"

"Hell, no. Satisfaction has definitely not been a part of my life since you buzzed into it. You're worse than a deranged gnat. Make that a whole swarm of gnats."

Somehow these unflattering words made Lindy feel better. Almost cheerful, in fact. She smiled at Nick in the last faint light of sundown. "See you later, Jarrett. The upheaval's only started. Remember that." And her little car, Sally, chugged away down the road, sounding quite cheerful itself.

THIS TIME Lindy left Hammersmith at home when she went to Nick's trailer. It had been quite a project getting out of her house. Hammers was catching on to her trick of tossing an apple into the living room to distract him. He'd learned to swallow the apple whole and then gallop after her before she was even out the door. This morning she'd thrown two apples into the living room. That had really flummoxed Hammers, because he hadn't known how to get both apples into his mouth at the same time. Now, as she knocked on the door of Nick's trailer, she made a mental note to buy another bag of apples at the produce mart.

Nick answered after several knocks, but didn't utter even one word of greeting. Perhaps he felt it was too early in the morning for speech. Lindy followed him into the kitchen. He hunched down in a chair at the small table, papers and file folders strewn all around him. Blueprints littered the floor at his feet, various cups and coffee mugs crowding each other on the chair beside him. The phone receiver was dangling from its cord; apparently Lindy had interrupted a conversation. Nick picked up the receiver, clamping it to his ear. He proceeded to demonstrate that he was quite capable of vociferous speech, even this early in the day.

"Dammit, I need to talk to Lowden himself. What kind of office are you running there, anyway? Hey, buddy, I don't care if he's in Tahiti. You have Lowden give me a call. Right away. Wait a minute, you can't hang up on me!" Nick took the receiver away from his ear and scowled at it. "Contractors," he muttered, then glanced up at Lindy. "Just what I need, on top of everything else. Another visit from the loony professor. I thought the town council meeting last week was punishment enough for both of us."

Lindy picked up one of the coffee mugs and sniffed the potent dregs inside it. "Goodness, you've been drinking coffee out of *all* these cups," she said in wonder.

"Yeah, well, so I like to start fresh with each pot. Is that a problem, or something?"

"You really are grouchy in the morning, aren't you? As a matter of fact, the Cluny wasn't much of a morning person, either. It just goes to show—"

"Wait a minute. Hold on. Don't start that with me."

"What are you talking about?"

"Professor, I can tell exactly what you've been doing ever since the Cluny crisis. A guy comes along, maybe you're attracted to him a little, maybe even a lot. Anyway, it scares you. So you start saying to yourself, 'This guy has a big nose, kind of like the Cluny's.' Or, 'This guy slurps his soup like the Cluny.' Then you're not attracted to him anymore, and you breathe easy again. That's what you're trying to pull with me—you're trying to put me on the Cluny black-list.''

Lindy grew furious as she listened to him. She dug into her purse, latching on to a chunk of obsidian. She had to rub her fingers over and over the glossy surface of the stone before she could regard Nick with any composure.

"Let me get this straight. You think I'm so all-fired attracted to you that it *scares* me?"

"Yes, that's what I think." Nick leaned back in his chair, arms folded across his broad chest. His eyes seemed very cool, the color of a New Mexico dusk.

Lindy ran her finger along the sharp edge of her obsidian. Yet, where she felt a real sharpness was inside her, as if Nick had cut through to the truth in her heart. She wanted to deny his words, but she couldn't.

"Jarrett, there's only one thing you have to know. I won't ever give another man the chance to betray me! Not ever. It hurt too darn much the first time. There's nothing wrong with trying to protect myself."

"Is that what you think I'd do—betray you? Lord, I'm not your Cluny. Stop trying to compare me to him. I'm straight with people. And I'm going to be straight with you, Lindy, right up front." He studied her, his eyes darkening. "Under any other circumstances, I'd take you in my arms about two seconds from now and I'd kiss you until neither one of us could remember what year it is. You're a damned desirable woman. You don't know it, but you are. I guess that's another legacy of the great Cluny—he made you doubt yourself."

Lindy had to delve into her purse for another rock, garnet this time. Longing thrummed in her at the mere thought of kissing Nick again. And he found her desirable, had said as much. She wanted to ponder this fascinating and disturbing bit of information. But Nick had gone on speaking.

"Maybe if you weren't so twisted around because of this Donald Cluny, things would be different. Maybe if you weren't so damn stubborn and didn't think you were right all the time. Heck, maybe if *everything* was different..." He shrugged and bent over his papers. "If you came here for a reason, state your business, Professor. Then get your tail feathers out of here. I have a lot of work to do."

Lindy dropped the obsidian and garnet back into her purse. This had gone way beyond rocks. You didn't tell a woman she was desirable, and the next minute dismiss her as if she was nothing but a nuisance!

Lindy remained obstinately where she was. Very well. Nick had made it quite evident he was attracted to her, but found her exasperating, aggravating and no end of trouble. Of course, that was exactly how she felt about him.

"You did come here for a reason, didn't you?" Nick grumbled. "Let's get on with it."

"I'm trying," she said. "But there's something different about you today." She circled behind him so she could get a good view from all angles. "Hmm... you got a haircut. It's nice. Although I liked the shaggy effect, I really did."

"It's a lousy haircut. Doesn't sit right." Nick put a hand on top of his head as if to make sure he hadn't been clipped bald.

"You must have paid a visit to the barbershop on Loma Street and had Fred take the shears to you. It looks like Fred's work, all right." Lindy gazed at the back of Nick's head. It seemed particularly vulnerable right now, the hair at his neckline clipped a mite too close. It made her think of cat fur, short yet soft and silky. She wiggled her fingers, wanting to run them over that gold-brown fuzz. Her hand inched toward Nick's head.

"Should've got my usual haircut in St. Louis," he said. "They don't know hair from prairie grass out here."

Lindy found the strength to withdraw her hand. Instead of stroking Nick's head, she wrapped her fingers around her purse strap. "Now, wait a minute. Fred may be a little overzealous, but he still does a fine job. In Santiago you can get as good a haircut as anywhere else."

"Ha. Give me a civilized barber in St. Louis any day—not some guy in the outback who goes bonkers with a pair of clippers."

Lindy glared at the back of Nick's head. "There's no place in the world like Santiago, New Mexico. And it takes a really civilized person to appreciate us here."

"Yeah, sure. I'd love to hear more about the glories of this town, but I have an airplane factory to build."

"Not at the moment, you don't." Lindy dived into her purse once more, rummaging around in it like an adventurous spelunker jumping into a cave. After a few moments she found what she was looking for—a letter that was only slightly crumpled after being wedged between her rocks. She shook some dirt off it and thrust it in front of Nick's nose. "Here, read this," she exclaimed in triumph. "It's a message for you from the planning office downtown. I offered to deliver it personally."

Nick unfolded the sheet of paper and rattled it suspiciously. He scanned the single typed paragraph. Lindy read along over his shoulder, even though she already knew the words by heart. After all, she'd dictated them herself late yesterday afternoon to Mary Beth down at the planning office. Goodness, though, Mary Beth ought to do something about the decrepit state of her typewriter; all the *e*'s and *o*'s danced above the line like undisciplined children.

"What the devil is this?" Nick demanded. "It says here—"

"It says you can't begin any construction on the factory because your site investigation report wasn't filed properly. That's what it says!"

Nick turned and scowled up at her. "Hold on. Those forms were filed months ago. If something was wrong with them, how come nobody objected until now?"

Lindy made a circuit of the kitchen. The room was so small she came full circle in a matter of seconds. "Unfortunately no one read your reports very carefully until I decided to study them. Turns out your engineers didn't provide a complete description on the test borings for the building foundation. I mean, it was pretty sloppy of them to keep writing in 'same as above,' 'same as above' all the time. That kind of vagueness and imprecision won't do at all."

Nick laughed incredulously. "You've got to be kidding. That's what this letter is all about?"

"Details are important in the engineering profession. You'll have to submit a completely new report, with everything filled out correctly." Lindy fidgeted with the box of coffee filters on the counter. She needed to sound calm and in control of this new scrimmage. The truth was it had been very difficult to convince Baxter Sloane at the planning office that Aldridge Aviation needed to file a new report. Baxter was like everyone else in town, wanting to give Aldridge the red-carpet treatment. It had taken Lindy forever to wear him down. She'd dictated the letter to Mary Beth and then dogged Baxter all around his office. He'd finally signed the letter just to get rid of her.

Now Lindy took one of the paper coffee filters and flattened it out on the counter. With its ruffled edges it reminded her of the tatted-lace doilies Aunt Eloise loved to make. "Jarrett, you do realize, of course, that you can't begin any construction on the factory until the engineering report is corrected."

Nick leaned back in his spindly chair and clasped his hands behind his head. This rumpled his newly shorn hair, making a clump of it poke up in back. "You're something else, Professor Mac. You probably spent hours going over that report, looking for some obscure technicality you could use against me. Any weapon, no matter how feeble."

She began marching again in the tight circle of the trailer's kitchen. "My weapons are strong enough. I got that letter signed, didn't I? And you have to abide by what it says."

"Sure. It's official—I'm not arguing with you there. But this is only a minor inconvenience for me. In twenty-four hours my people will have another report at the planning office, and this time even you won't be able to find fault with it.''

Lindy had known all along she'd be causing Nick only a short delay. But it was the best she could do. ''Very well, then! Give those twenty-four hours to me. Put yourself in my hands—let me prove to you that what you're doing is wrong.'' She brought her fist down on the counter for emphasis, making the coffeepot rattle.

''Forget it, Professor. I'm not going to listen to any more of your preaching.''

Lindy forced herself to answer in a calm, measured voice. ''You won't get any speeches from me, I can promise you that. What I want to do is... well, you'll just have to trust me. Turn yourself over to me completely for the next twenty-four hours.'' She paused, rather overwhelmed by her own proposal. It would be daunting, spending all that time with Nick when she didn't know whether she wanted to kiss him or dump a pile of rocks on his head.

Nick went on leaning back in his chair. ''No way, Professor. I don't like the sound of this at all. Besides, there's still plenty of paperwork I can take care of today, and telephone calls I can make—''

''You can't do anything related to business,'' Lindy insisted. ''In a strictly legal sense, that engineering report has to be refiled before anything else happens with the factory. Baxter Sloane and the entire planning office will back me on this, I'm warning you!'' Lindy didn't mention that her greatest support at the planning office came from Mary Beth, the part-time secretary.

Nick straightened up and drummed his fingers thoughtfully on the table. He surprised Lindy with a slow grin. "You know, Linden Eloise, we might be able to reach a compromise here. I'll give you twenty-four hours—as long as you promise me one thing."

"What?" she asked warily.

"After the twenty-four hours are up, you won't ever bug me again about those owls. The subject will be closed, once and for all."

Lindy was indignant. "You can't ask me to make a promise like that! I'm going to fight you to the very end, Jarrett—"

"Whoa. You need to learn how to bargain for what you want. You'll get a lot more accomplished that way. Think about it. I give you twenty-four hours—you promise to leave me in peace for the rest of my natural life. What could be more fair?"

Lindy fumed. His offer wasn't fair in the least. "No," she stated flatly. "I won't compromise on something this important."

Nick shrugged. "Too bad. You'll never have another opportunity like this one. All that time to convince me to change my mind. What's the matter, Professor? Don't you have any faith in your own abilities?"

Blast him! He was ridiculing her again. From his tone it was evident *he* didn't have any faith in her powers of persuasion. Goaded by Nick, Lindy began to feel reckless. She faced him, keeping one hand behind her back so she could cross her fingers.

"All right, Jarrett. We have a deal. Give me the next twenty-four hours, and I won't bother you anymore after that."

"Hey, you're giving in too easily. And what are you doing with your hand back there?"

"Nothing."

"You're crossing your fingers, aren't you?" Nick shook his head. "And I thought you were a woman of integrity, Eloise."

Lindy's cheeks flamed. She held both hands out in front of her. "Okay, okay. See? I'm not crossing any fingers now."

"What about toes?"

"Oh, good grief. I'm wearing hiking boots. I couldn't cross my toes even if I tried."

Nonetheless, Nick craned his head so he could examine her feet. "Hmm . . . seems legitimate. Give me your solemn oath that you're not going to fudge on our deal."

"You're making this into a joke. You're not taking it seriously at all."

Nick raised his eyebrows and put on an expression of affronted innocence. "I'm not the one crossing my fingers behind my back so I can tell fibs. I'm going to live up to my part of the agreement. I'll give you my undivided attention until exactly—" he checked his watch "—eight twenty-three tomorrow morning. What more could you want?"

Lindy hesitated, still holding her hands out in front of her. To stake everything on the next twenty-four hours—no, it was too much to ask! But would she have any chance to influence Nick otherwise? She was fast running out of options in her campaign against Aldridge Aviation. Certainly she couldn't afford to lose this one.

"The clock's ticking," Nick remarked. "Let me see, it's eight twenty-six now."

"No—wait. We don't start counting until I say yes to the deal. And I say...yes." Lindy let out her breath in a whoosh. She'd done it—committed herself to Nick's terms. She had no choice but to come through for the owls. "From right this minute your time is mine," she declared. "Let's get started—"

"As soon as I make one phone call. I'm going to make darn sure that new engineering report is ready by tomorrow. Don't worry, we won't start our countdown until I'm finished with the call. I told you I'd be fair about this, didn't I?"

Lindy watched impatiently as Nick punched out a number on the phone. He seemed to think his day with her would be a diversion, nothing more, and then he could get back to business as usual with that wretched airplane factory. Well, he was wrong. It wasn't going to work out that way. Somehow she'd make him understand, make him change his point of view.

Lindy shifted the load of her purse from one shoulder to the other. She couldn't afford to waste one precious moment now that she had Nick Jarrett all to herself. Still, she had seized this opportunity in desperation, with only half-formed plans in mind. Summer session at the college was over now, and she didn't have any classes to teach. She was free to devote herself solely to Nick's education. But where should she begin? Which tactic would be absolutely the best?

"Listen, Tom, I know it doesn't make any sense," Nick was saying into the phone. "The report was fine first time around. But this crazy geologist person has influence in town. More than I'd given her credit for...

Don't get bent out of shape, will you? We're going to comply and refile the report. Less delay involved that way. Look, Tom, nobody's questioning your integrity, and nobody's saying you're dumb. I know what your IQ is. I don't want to hear about it again. Just get to work on that report.''

Nick slammed the receiver down in its cradle, all his morning grumpiness back full force. He stalked over to the counter, picking up the empty coffeepot and shaking it upside down. A few drops of murky brown liquid dribbled out, but that was all. Nick frowned at the pot.

''Why is everybody giving me trouble this morning?'' he complained.

Lindy took the pot from him, setting it back in the coffeemaker. ''You're tense. That's your real problem. Look at the way your shoulders are all bunched up.''

''I'm not tense, dammit!''

Lindy jiggled one of his arms. It was stiff and unyielding.

''For goodness' sake, relax your muscles,'' she commanded. She lifted his arm until it jutted straight out from his side, then she allowed it to fall back down again. No good; the arm was still as rigid as a slab of marble. Lindy shook her head. ''What are you thinking about?'' she asked.

Nick drew his eyebrows together. ''I'm thinking how every detail of this factory project is turning into a royal pain in the neck.''

''Well, that's it, exactly. I can see you clenching your neck muscles from here. Think about something else. Like flying in an airplane, up there in the clouds with no one to aggravate you."

"No one like you, Professor?" Nick remarked dryly. But his eyes looked wistful. "Lord, it's been a long time since I flew just for fun. That's all I ever wanted, to fly planes, tear loose from the ground..." He gazed out the small window of the trailer to the bright southwestern sky beyond.

After a long moment Lindy ventured to prod his arm. Much better this time. Now there was definitely some give in Nick's muscles; he'd started to relax.

Lindy smiled. Suddenly she knew exactly how she would proceed with Nick today. She knew what he needed in his life, even if he didn't realize it himself. She had to show him. It was as simple as that. Concentrate on Nick first, and then...well, the rest of it would follow naturally.

"Start the countdown," she said softly. "Twenty-four hours, Jarrett, on the nose. I'm ready."

CHAPTER SIX

NICK DIDN'T ANSWER. He went on gazing out the window as if any moment a whole squadron of airplanes would appear. Lindy studied him critically. Today he was wearing another pair of expensive, well-tailored trousers and a dress shirt with a button-down collar. Even the shirt pockets were kept severely closed with their own subdued buttons. The creases in his clothes were fading, as if he wasn't living out of a suitcase so much anymore. He looked every bit a business executive. That wouldn't do at all.

Lindy headed for the door. "It's obvious what we have to do first. Very obvious. Come with me." She led the way out of the trailer. Nick followed his own path, going over to his truck.

"We're taking my car," she informed him, swinging open the passenger door. "Hop in."

"Forget it. You drive an impressive antique there, but in case you haven't noticed, it's full of rocks. I still can't figure out how you manage to squeeze the wonder dog in."

Lindy was adamant. "We're taking my car. There's plenty of room. And today you need to be completely separated from your usual environment. You need to be totally ready for the new and unexpected."

"Isn't that how brainwashing works? Disorient people by taking them out of familiar surroundings, then try to reprogram their minds? Afraid that won't work with me, Professor Mac."

Lindy didn't listen. She'd already dropped her purse and was hauling a large chunk of granite from the floor of the car. Nick moved to help her, but she held on to the rock.

"I'm fine," she panted. "I got it in here by myself—I'll get it out."

Now they were both crouched in awkward positions by the car, the rock a precarious load between them. Nick began tugging the rock away from Lindy.

"Let go," he commanded. "You're always tussling with me over something or other and causing no end of problems...eegah!" Nick toppled over backward, taking the rock with him. He ended up flat on the ground, his limbs sprawled every which way, the rock plunking down on his stomach and remaining there like a bizarre monument.

Lindy scrambled over to him, dragging the rock off his body. "Are you all right? Can you talk? Can you move?"

He gazed up at her. The clear, intense blue of his irises startled Lindy. His attractiveness was always taking her by surprise; she couldn't get used to it. Right now all she could do was gaze back at him. He didn't speak, and perhaps the wind had been knocked clean out of him. But then, reaching up his hands, he cupped Lindy's face and brought it down to his own. He kissed her.

The touch of his lips was simple and matter-of-fact. It was a basic kiss, no unnecessary frills—the perfect kiss to receive from a man who was sprawled in the dirt among sagebrush and piñon trees. The sun shone warm and brilliant, dazzling Lindy. Or maybe she was dazzled by Nick. She swayed as he kissed her and nearly went tumbling into his arms. At the last moment she rescued herself, breaking away from him and sitting up straight. She pushed back her tousled hair.

"Hey," she said. She couldn't say more because her breathing was too uneven.

"Hey what?" Nick stretched in the dirt and clasped his hands behind his head. He smiled like a man well satisfied. And somehow that made Lindy just plain mad.

"You said you weren't going to do anything like this! You said the circumstances weren't right. You said—"

"It was an unpremeditated kiss. And besides, it was your fault. You looked inviting."

So now she was desirable *and* inviting. That seemed an appealing combination, like finding two good minerals together in a rock. But it wouldn't do to get carried away by this new vision of herself. Lindy cleared her throat and patted her hair. It was crackling with electricity in the oddest fashion.

"Now, listen. You kissing me and vice versa isn't part of the deal today. It's too distracting."

"Let's try vice versa for a change. We'll measure how distracting it is on a scale of one to ten." Nick's smile broadened into a grin. He had good teeth, no doubt about it. But was that any reason for Lindy's heart to thump in her chest like twenty pistons gone out of sync?

She struggled to her feet, brushing off the knees of her khaki pants. Nick remained spread out on the ground.

"Aren't you going to help me up?" he asked, humor spiking his voice. He held out his hand to her.

Lindy examined that outstretched hand suspiciously. She'd be a fool to take hold of it. Still, he had almost been flattened by her rock. Maybe he really needed some assistance.

She allowed his fingers to grasp hers. With one smooth motion he pulled her down beside him again. Her legs tangled with his. She was cradled against his chest, her mouth only a whisper away from his own. She could feel the laughter rumbling inside him as his arms tightened around her. But this time there was no kiss, and gradually Nick's laughter faded. He and Lindy stared at each other, both of them solemn.

"Dammit, Professor, don't look at me like that," he said, his voice husky.

"Like how?" she whispered.

"Like no one's ever held you or kissed you the right way before. But you're so beautiful any guy would start aching for you."

He was making her feel beautiful for the first time in her life. "Nick . . ."

"Yes?" His breath fanned her cheek, warm and fresh.

"The truth is . . . nobody's ever kissed me the way you do. Not the Cluny, not anyone."

"If I keep on kissing you, we're both in trouble. You know that, don't you?"

"Big trouble."

"Very big trouble." His lips brushed hers for barely a second. It was a promise unfulfilled, a taste of delight just out of reach. She lost herself in Nick's eyes and knew that if she didn't watch herself, here was a man she could care about. No matter how much she disagreed with him, no matter how much she hated his wretched airplane factory, he touched something deep inside her—some layer of emotion that had lain undisturbed for years, like cooled magma. Nick was bringing warmth to her. Oh, yes, she could care for him. And then she'd truly be lost....

As if by mutual agreement, she and Nick rolled apart. They sat side by side on the ground. Nick shook his head with obvious perplexity.

"You get under my skin in too many ways, Professor. Are you ever going to stop?"

"You're the one who has to stop." Lindy reminded herself that Nick Jarrett was the *last* man she could afford to go soft over. But that was exactly how she felt around him. Soft and womanly. And he was right—it scared her to bits.

"Have you noticed something?" she asked, attempting a light tone. "Whenever you and I start to travel anywhere together, we don't make much progress at all."

"Are you still determined to haul me around in your limousine? Sadie, or whatever the heck its name is." Nick massaged the shorn back of his neck as if trying to stimulate hair growth.

"Sally. Her name is Sally. And there's only one more rock in front of the passenger seat."

"Don't move. I'll take care of this one strictly on my own."

Lindy didn't argue with him. She needed a few minutes to reorder her thoughts. But as Nick heaved the rock out of the car, she never got beyond admiring the flex and pull of his muscles. The man put her in a dangerous state, and she had to do something about it. Soon!

She stood as he started to settle himself in the passenger seat. "Wait a minute," she called. "We can't just leave my rocks out here in the open. Someone might steal them."

"You've got to be kidding. Who's going to want a couple of crummy rocks?"

"These are fine specimens," Lindy said indignantly. "Just look at the mica sparkling in that granite. I mean, someone could come walking along here and see all those lovely speckles glittering in the sun, and that would be it. Anyone can get carried away by mica, you know. It has that effect on people—"

"All right, all right," Nick groaned. "Don't tell me any more. I'll put the darn rocks on the top step of the trailer, safely away from all those mica fiends out there."

"No, that's not good enough. We'll have to put the rocks inside your trailer. How else will they be completely safe?"

Nick shook his head. "I know you're not serious. Nobody could be serious about something like this. Come on, Professor. Tell me you're pulling my leg."

Lindy flushed. Nick was looking at her like she was nuts. But she was serious. Why shouldn't she be? There was nothing in the world as wonderful as rocks.

With a resigned expression, Nick stepped out of the car and picked up her chunk of granite. She ran to help him. By the time they'd carted it to the trailer both were bent over with the weight of the rock. And then they got stuck in the narrow doorway.

"Rotate to your left," Nick commanded.

"No. *You* go left. That's the only way."

"Do you always think you're right about everything, Professor?"

"Only when I'm right. And this time I'm right. Go left!"

Somehow they both ended up going left, careening together through the doorway. The rock plummeted to the floor with a terrible crash, barely missing Nick's toes.

"Good Lord," he muttered. "That's it. No more rocks. The other one stays outside. End of story."

"But, Nick—"

"Eloise, I've spent roughly half an hour in your company this morning, and already I'm going crazy. Loony, loopy, berserk. That's me. What do you think I'm going to be like at the end of twenty-four hours?"

"You're the one who drives *me* crazy," Lindy protested. "You make me feel demented, deranged and just plain distracted!"

"Unhinged, unbalanced, unsettled," Nick grumbled as he stalked outside. "Try to outdo that."

"Balmy, buggy, bananas..."

"All right, all right, I give up." At the bottom of the steps, Nick turned around and jabbed his finger toward the middle of the trailer. "See? It's beginning to sag. All that extra weight from your rock has done the place in. Looks no better than a swaybacked horse with a sagging belly. What have I gotten myself into? That's what I'd like to know."

Lindy stared hard at the trailer. Was it sagging, just a bit? Oh, of course not. She lingered for a moment next to her other rock, wishing she could tuck it safely inside the trailer, too. But something told her not to press her luck. She grabbed her purse and slid into the driver's seat of her little blue car. She waited until Nick folded his rangy frame into the seat beside her before she started the engine. At first Sally coughed and stuttered like a delicate old lady with a cold. But a few minutes later she smoothed into a steady hum, showing how sturdy and dependable she was.

"Boy, this is some car," Nick said. "It even sounds like an airplane."

Lindy glanced at him sharply. "Are you being sarcastic? Because there's no reason to be sarcastic about Sally. No reason at all."

"I'm being one hundred percent sincere. They don't make cars like this anymore. These seat belts are strong enough to hold down an ox. And look at the panoramic view out the windows. Say, you even have a hat rack in here." Nick gestured at Lindy's baseball cap, which was dangling from the gearshift knob. She took the cap and crammed it onto her head. As for the windows, they were panoramic, all right, but they were also smeared from Hammersmith's exuberant tongue. Hammers never could seem to sit still when he came along for a ride; he always had to have his nose pressed against one window or another. Lindy wished fervently that she had some paper towels and glass cleaner, anything to destroy the evidence of Hammersmith's unruly behavior.

"Um, roll down your window," she improvised. "All the way. You need some fresh country air in your lungs. Take a big gulp of it. Doesn't that feel great?"

"Lord, what I really need is another cup of coffee."

Lindy wasn't daunted by Nick's lack of enthusiasm. She was starting to think a little clearer. Her strategy for the day was taking more shape and direction by the minute.

Eager to put her plans into action, Lindy went from neutral to first gear. Unfortunately Sally had a stubborn clutch and sometimes she needed a little coaxing. Nick didn't say anything as Lindy wrestled with the stick shift. He didn't have to say anything. His amusement was almost palpable.

At last the car lurched forward. Second gear and even third were achieved with only minor struggles. Sally chugged down the road. Nick's trailer was situated well on the outskirts of Santiago, and the road wound past small farms and fields where cattle grazed. The fields were a vivid lush green, fed by the waters of the Rio Grande. Even the cows had a luxuriant texture, their hides a glossy brown and white.

It was only a short while before Lindy arrived in the downtown area of Santiago. She drove extra slowly around the plaza, with its gazebo and Spanish urns. She wanted to be sure Nick realized what a beautiful little town this was. But all he did was yawn, right in front of the prettiest bed of purple irises he could ever hope to see. Lindy wasn't discouraged; after all, the day had only begun. She ended her scenic tour by parking at Beckett's Surplus and Supply. Then she hurried out of the car.

"Come on," she called over her shoulder. "We're going to shop and get some better clothes for you.... Wait a minute, where are you going? Come back here!"

Nick was moving at such a good clip he was halfway down the street before Lindy caught up to him. She latched onto his arm, but even that didn't stop his momentum. He tried to shake her off.

"Listen, Professor, you're going too far. I've never gone shopping for clothes with a woman, and I'm not about to start now."

Lindy hung on to him, dragging her feet over the sidewalk in an effort to slow him down. "You don't have any choice. You have to wear something else today."

Nick stopped abruptly, and Lindy almost went flying off his arm. But she managed to stay clamped to him. He scowled at her. "What the heck is wrong with the clothes I'm wearing?"

"They're fine if you want to look like a corporate executive who's about to go bore himself silly in a business meeting. But where you and I are headed ... Well, when we get there you'll understand why you need to wear something special. Come on, I'm only asking you to do a little shopping."

"I don't shop. I hate to shop. I'd rather bang myself over the head with a frying pan than shop. You got that?"

"Goodness." Lindy thought about this for a moment. "Then how do all these business clothes end up in your closet? I mean, do they just fly in through the window somehow, flapping their sleeves?"

Nick glared at her. "I have a system. A store in St. Louis delivers clothes right to my doorstep. Everything I need. No hassle, no bother, no salespeople following me around and driving me crazy—like you drive me crazy! That's my system, and it's not going to change." Nick folded his arms across his chest, his posture unyielding. Lindy was still hanging on to him like a stubborn leach. A few passersby looked over with curious glances, but she was determined not to give up.

"I'm impressed with this system of yours," she told Nick. "Really I am. Clothes delivered to your house like so many pizzas. I see the appeal in that. But I think your problem is that you've never shopped at the right store. You don't know what shopping can be like under the proper circumstances. Let me introduce you to the total shopping experience."

"Forget it."

"You don't understand," she said earnestly. "You need to wear the right clothes today. It's absolutely essential!"

"I don't shop. And that's a matter of principle. You believe in sticking to your principles, so you should understand how I feel."

Apparently they were at an impasse, but Lindy wouldn't let go of Nick. They were standing in front of the plate-glass windows of Geneva's Laundromat, their reflection shining back at them: Nick with his arms folded, Lindy dangling from him at an awkward angle. They looked like they'd gotten stuck together with glue, and didn't know how to get unstuck again. Geneva herself had come to the other side of the window, waving her hand cheerfully at Lindy. Unfortunately Lindy couldn't wave back because that would mean loosening her grip on Nick. She waggled her foot up and down, hoping that would convey an appropriate greeting. Then she started working on Nick again.

"Seems to me we have an agreement, Jarrett. We made a deal. You were supposed to turn yourself over to me completely for twenty-four hours. Are you already trying to worm your way out?"

"I always live up to my agreements. But you never said anything about shopping."

"Well, you never told me you had this thing about shopping. To be fair, you should have warned me beforehand. The truth is you didn't put any restrictions to our deal. Any lawyer would back me up."

They stared at each other in a silent battle of wills. Lindy pulled on Nick. He advanced one step, then another. He stopped.

"Twenty-four hours," she murmured. "And after that I'll never bother you again. Of course, if you don't live up to your end of the agreement, I can hound you all I want. You'll see Hammersmith and me everywhere you turn." She pulled on him again, dragging him forward a few more steps. They were starting to leave Geneva's Laundromat behind. Geneva waved again, looking forlorn now, as if she didn't want to see them go.

Lindy pulled Nick all the way down to Beckett's Surplus and Supply. She even got him through the door before he put on the brakes again. Calvin Beckett, Sr., came out from behind his cash register. As usual, Calvin was wearing army fatigues that were at least two sizes too large for his small, wiry body. His pants were all bunched up over his boots. He looked like a jockey outfitted as a soldier.

"Hello there, Teach," he greeted Lindy, his voice thin and reedy. Then he turned to Nick. "I know who you are. You're that fella who's goin' to build our new factory. Tell you what. Calvin, Jr.'s lookin' for a job. Smart boy, Calvin, Jr. Helps me out in the store. The boy can do anything. What say I send him over to you?"

Lindy sighed. It seemed everyone in town, without exception, was gung ho about Aldridge Aviation. And Nick, in spite of his aversion to shopping, was quite genial to Calvin.

"When we start hiring workers, have your son fill out an application. I'm sure we can find a place for him."

Calvin, Sr., nodded. "You a navy man?"

"No..."

"Army?"

"Not that, either," Nick admitted.

Calvin was beginning to look doubtful. "Marines? Air Force?"

"I fly airplanes. Does that count?"

"It's good enough, I reckon. Woulda been an army man myself, except this bum knee kept me out." Then Calvin ran a hand over his balding head and studied Nick's hair. "Took yourself down to Fred for a barber job, didn't you? Too bad. Somebody shoulda warned you off Fred."

Nick rubbed the nape of his neck, obviously perturbed. He started backing toward the door.

"Calvin, Mr. Jarrett here needs a camouflage shirt," Lindy said hastily. "Could you pick one out for us? You'd better hurry! And a pair of camouflage pants, too, while you're at it.'' Nick was already half-way out the door, dragging Lindy with him. She looked speculatively at a coil of rope on one of the shelves. Maybe she could reach it somehow, and lasso Nick.... No, too hazardous, by far. If she let go of him for even a second, she'd lose him. It was better to keep hanging on to him for dear life.

Fortunately, Calvin, Sr. seemed to understand this was something of an emergency. Lindy knew he'd trained himself for years to think like a soldier in bat-tle, and now he went into action. He sped down an aisle, and sped back again in record time with the pants and shirt.

"I guarantee these are the right size, Teach."

"Good. That's good. Now, all we have to do is get him into the dressing room. You take his other arm, and when I count three . . .''

Nick gave her a look sour enough to turn cucum-bers into pickles. He grabbed the clothes and strode back toward the dressing room on his own.

"I think we have him now, if we just leave him alone," Lindy whispered to Calvin.

"Got you, Teach. This operation is goin' to be suc-cessful. You can count on me."

Together they peered cautiously around a shelf and watched Nick disappear into the dressing room. They listened as a spate of grumbling came from the room, along with an inordinate amount of banging.

"Do you think he's hitting the walls?" Lindy asked.

"Hard to tell. Could be. Let's sit tight. We'll storm him later if we have to."

"You keep on the lookout. I'm going to make a foray for a hat. He definitely needs a hat, but I want to take him by surprise."

Lindy sprinted down the aisle, past a jumble of duffel bags, tents, tarps, canteens, mess kits and ponchos. Her purse bumped against her hip as she ran. She'd browsed through this store so many times she knew right where to head. She snatched a safari hat, size medium, and then paused by a display of boots. She picked out a good solid pair of chukka ankle boots that looked like they'd fit Nick. Certainly they'd be much more practical for where they were going than his expensive loafers.

Lindy headed back to take her position beside Calvin. "I'll switch shoes on Nick when I get a chance," she whispered. "Meanwhile, I've got to hide these boots somewhere." Thinking fast, she dumped several of the biggest rocks out of her purse and crammed the boots in there. It took some effort to zip up the purse again, but Lindy managed it. She'd merely exchanged one type of bulge for another, and Nick would be none the wiser. "Take care of my rocks, will you, Calvin? All we have to do is get this hat on him, and we'll have it made."

"Sounds like he's comin' out," Calvin warned. "You be ready to make your move."

The dressing-room door banged open. Nick emerged in the camouflage clothes, looking thoroughly out of sorts. Lindy crouched in readiness with the hat.

"Now!" said Calvin. Lindy darted forward, clapping the hat on Nick's head before he knew what hit him. Then she seized his hand and made a beeline for the front door.

"Thanks, Calvin. Just put these things on my bill. We'll pick up his other clothes later. So long!"

Calvin gave her a thumbs-up. She hauled Nick out of the store in triumph. Her plan was working superbly. She'd already accomplished step number one.

Of course, there was a minor problem. It seemed Nick didn't appreciate her efforts. He stopped in the middle of the sidewalk and glared at Lindy. The expression on his face was so ominous it was a wonder puffs of steam didn't start billowing out his ears.

"All right," he said grimly. "Suppose you tell me about it. Tell me why the heck I look like this all of a sudden. Like I'm about to go hide out in a jungle somewhere and fight guerrillas. Just tell me why, Eloise!" he ended on a bellow.

And now Lindy could swear she almost *did* see steam wafting in outrage from Nick Jarrett's ears.

CHAPTER SEVEN

"IN A LITTLE WHILE you'll understand everything, Nick. And the truth is, you really do look good in camouflage. Let yourself get used to it, that's all. Pretty soon you'll want to dress like this all the time." Lindy feared that any minute Nick was going to explode, rather like an overheated boiler. If only he realized how truly wonderful he looked in all those variegated swirls of green and brown and black. His powerful build was emphasized by the rugged attire. And the safari hat had landed on his head at a lopsided but debonair angle. Altogether, he made Lindy think of adventure—adventure, excitement and risks she'd never taken before....

She experienced a startling temptation to throw her arms around Nick and kiss him, right there on Main Street. But she suspected he wouldn't take too kindly to such a gesture.

"I think we'd better do more shopping," she decided. Before Nick could start bellowing again, she held up her hand. "We're going to buy some food, that's all. You do shop for food, don't you? Or is that against your principles, too?"

It turned out that once Nick got his hands on a grocery cart, he zoomed around the store with it like he was doing laps on the Indianapolis Speedway. Lindy had to jog to keep up with him. Her purse swung in a new rhythm, bulkier than usual with Nick's pair of boots, but still a pleasant weight hanging from her shoulder. She took a package of cheese and tossed it into the grocery cart as it whizzed past her. Then she aimed a box of crackers at the cart and missed. Scooping the box off the floor, she ran after Nick.

"Do you prefer root beer, grape juice or cherry soda?" she panted.

"Anything." He reached out, randomly grabbed a jar of peanut butter and chucked it into the cart—all without breaking stride. Lindy went back for a six-pack of grape juice. Afterward she took a shortcut by darting into the next aisle, heading off Nick as he came charging down it.

"Your grocery-store technique is a disgrace," she told him. "I mean, you're supposed to read labels and comparison shop. Make informed decisions!"

Nick's eyes held a dangerous glint as he veered the cart around Lindy. "I'm showing you the right way to do groceries. Pay attention, and you might learn a thing or two." Without even looking at what he was doing, he threw a bag of corn chips and a box of raisins into the cart in quick succession.

"You know, shopping with you is like trying to walk an ornery cat on a leash," she complained. But even as she spoke, Nick's cart left her in the dust.

They emerged from the store in record time, laden with two large bags of groceries. Nick frowned at Lindy over the top of his sack.

"I'm done. No more confounded shopping. I've reached my limit. You got that, Professor? I don't care what our deal is. From here on out it's no stores, no malls, no bargain warehouses, no fruit stands, nothing.''

"Don't get yourself all worked up. We're done shopping."

"You'd better believe it," he muttered, rattling his grocery sack as if for emphasis.

Lindy smiled. "It's time," she said.

"Time for what?"

"Time for us to go."

"Go where?"

"The place where we're going."

Nick made a noise that was somewhere between a groan and a howl, sounding rather like one of Hammersmith's tirades. "You're really going to do it to me. You're going to drive me insane. I'll never make it twenty-four hours. Never."

"Yes, you will," Lindy said confidently. She was pleased she could shake him up this way. It meant she had some influence on him, no matter how perverse.

Yes, it was definitely time for the next move.

LINDY PARKED SALLY at the end of a dirt road. Rummaging around in the back seat, she found her heavy-duty knapsack wedged behind a hunk of sandstone. She dusted off the knapsack and proceeded to stuff the groceries into it.

Nick watched all this with a lugubrious expression. "I don't know what damn fool idea you have in mind, but you'd better let me carry that." He pulled the straps of the knapsack over his shoulders. "Whatever we're going to do, let's get on with it."

Lindy liked him in a knapsack, his shoulders broad and capable of carrying the load. She was doing almost too good a job of outfitting him; his appeal was growing by the minute. And that made it so she couldn't think straight again. She pressed a hand to her forehead. No doubt about it—she was suffering from Jarrett fever. Somehow she had to keep it under control. She was on a mission today, and she needed all her wits about her to accomplish it successfully.

Turning away from Nick, she took a few deep breaths of air to clear her head. Darn it! Even when she wasn't looking at him, his image was imprinted in her mind like an etching in stone. Hair golden brown like the feathers of a hawk's wing, eyes an intense blue...

But it was more than that. It wasn't merely Nick's physical attractiveness. There was something deeper in him that drew her. She sensed the good solid core of his personality—something trustworthy at his very center. Slowly she was beginning to believe what he'd told her about himself this morning. Surely Nick Jarrett would never pretend to be something he wasn't. And he wouldn't hesitate to let a person know exactly how he felt; all his emotions were blunt and straightforward, none of the edges softened. Lindy had discovered that much already.

"Are we going somewhere, or what?" he demanded behind her.

"I'm almost ready." Lindy dived back into the car, searching distractedly for her camera. She didn't really want to believe so many good things about Nick Jarrett. Because she had also believed good things about the Cluny. For years she'd given him all the loyalty in her nature. In return he had favored her with that one big, whopping betrayal. Hadn't she learned anything? Did she honestly believe she could jump right in and trust Nick, after knowing him such a short while?

She found her camera, as well as her binoculars. But she backed out of the car too fast, hitting her head on the door frame.

"Ouch!"

"Lord, you really knocked yourself there. Let me see." Nick strode over to her. Before she could stop him, he took off her baseball cap and put it on the roof of the car. Then he started probing her skull.

"I'm fine. You don't need to do this," she protested. Yet even as she spoke, she delighted in the warm, gentle touch of Nick's big hands. She felt as if she was receiving a strange and lovely benediction.

"Hmm...everything seems to be all right." He ran his fingers through her tumble of hair. "I guarantee you won't suffer any permanent damage from that bump to your noggin. But watch where you're going."

"I usually do." Lindy stepped away and pressed her baseball cap back on her head. She swung her binoculars crosswise over one shoulder, her camera over the other. With her purse also in place, she had a whole network of straps on her body.

She gazed up at Nick. Reluctantly, she admitted to herself that her entire plan for the day was based on trust in one form or another. She trusted her ability to show Nick what he lacked in his life; she believed she could convince him that helping her would be to his own advantage. Even more than that, she trusted in his basic core of decency. She had faith that his decency, if nothing else, would make him want to protect those little owls. Yes, it was scary, trusting him so much. But she had no other choice.

"Why are you looking at me like I just grew a second nose?" he asked. "If you're going to say anything about my haircut, forget it. I've already heard enough."

Lindy started marching through a spiny thicket of mesquite. "The way I look at it, hair always grows out."

Nick was close at her heels. "Thanks. I feel a lot better now. You've really cheered me up."

"Well, you're the one who brought it up in the first place. And it does grow out, you know."

They hiked together over the broad mesa, scrub and cactus thick around them. Desert grasses stirred in the breeze, and wildflowers gave vivid, unexpected flashes of violet and gold. Lindy had parked quite a distance from the destination she had in mind. She wanted Nick to travel by foot so he would be close to the subtle beauty of this land right away. But it didn't take him long to figure out where they were going.

"Wait a minute. We're headed straight for the factory site."

"That's right."

"You're wasting your time, Professor. You're not going to show me anything I haven't already seen. I spend half my time out there."

"Maybe so, but today you're going to see it from my perspective. That's going to make all the difference. All the difference in the world."

"I've been over every inch of that terrain. Heck, I could show *you* a thing or two."

"We'll see," Lindy said quietly. She didn't speak anymore as they went on. This was a landscape for silence. The sky was brilliant and cloudless, as pure as sapphire. In the distance, the mountains rose against the horizon like a strong and protective rampart. Close by, the earth had eroded into delicate ridges and gullies; Lindy thought of this as her own miniature Grand Canyon. Then the mesa spread out again. Lindy swung into a loose, easy stride, so sure and familiar with this land that she could have found her way even at midnight. And there was the factory site, unmarred as yet by the presence of tractors or building crews. She led Nick to her special place, a rough indentation in the ground with a few boulders scattered about. A single young juniper tree offered the idea of shade, if not the reality.

Nick glanced around. "I'm telling you, this is nothing new. We're going to level out this section here. It'll end up being part of the runway for test flights."

Lindy clenched her hands on her binoculars. "None of that has happened yet. This isn't a runway—it's my foxhole, the way it's always been."

"Your what?" Laughter danced at the corners of Nick's mouth.

"My own private foxhole, blast it."

"Eloise, you've been spending way too much time at the army-surplus store. Next you'll start saying we really are going to fight some guerrillas. Are we supposed to dive for cover in case of enemy fire? I guess this camouflage stuff will come in handy, after all." He chuckled.

Lindy untangled her purse and camera straps. "Laugh all you like. But if you'll sit down and keep a

lid on it, you'll find out soon enough why camouflage is so important out here.''

He looked belligerent, as if he was going to start
arguing with her again. Instead, he surprised her by
slipping the knapsack off his shoulders and sitting
down as instructed. He didn't seem comfortable,
though. He kept shifting position, his knees jutting
first in one direction and then another.

Lindy tried to give him a lesson in the art of sitting
outdoors. She sank gracefully onto the ground, then
pulled up her knees and clasped them. She settled into
immediate stillness, the breeze whispering around her.
Nick watched her quizzically. After shifting around
some more, he sat cross-legged and hunched his
shoulders in an awkward pose. Lindy supposed that
was the best she could expect from him. When he
seemed about to speak, she lifted a cautionary finger
to her lips. And then she pointed to a spot some yards
away.

The tawny owl stood tall and straight on his mound,
his yellow eyes luminous and unblinking. His color-
ing was intricate, feathers all speckled white as if he'd
been caught in a summer snowstorm. With his small
body perched on slender legs, he reminded Lindy of a
little man dressed in skinny, high-waisted trousers. He
stared at Nick and Lindy, his brow furrowed in what
appeared to be permanent disapproval of intruders.
After a moment his head swiveled far to the left, and
then to the right. He seemed to be hoping that when
he looked forward again, Nick and Lindy would have
vanished. Finally he started to bob up and down in a
rapid, jerky motion, like someone doing calisthenics
and wanting to get them over with in a hurry.

"WHEE-whee-whee-whee-whee," he called in a raspy voice. "WHEE-whee-whee-whee-whee!"

Lindy handed the binoculars over to Nick. "He's acting as sentry," she whispered. "He's warning the others about us and letting us know just whose territory this is."

Nick stared through the binoculars. "I didn't know owls came out during the daytime," he said, his own voice a low murmur. "I've never seen one when I've been here before."

"I told you that you'd see something new with me. You have to be looking for owls. You have to want to see them."

No matter how the sentry chided them, Nick and Lindy remained stubbornly seated in the foxhole. After a while other owls gradually emerged from their burrows, taking wing or standing guard at their own mounds. They were used to Lindy by now, and perhaps because of that willing to tolerate Nick. He trained the binoculars on one owl as it wheeled in the sky above him.

"Intriguing," he murmured. "Small tail feathers, but look at the spread of those wings. They don't make any noise when they fly, either. Not a rustle or a flap. Reminds me of a glider I used to have."

"The owls are beautiful, aren't they? And they're smart, too. You know, they didn't waste any time digging those burrows themselves. They took them over from prairie dogs. If that isn't clever, I don't know what is."

Nick lowered the binoculars. "What do you expect me to say, Lindy? I think your owls are fine. They're great. Is that supposed to change anything?"

"All I want you to do is enjoy yourself. Tell me. Are your clothes comfortable?"

Nick began rolling up his sleeves. "Yeah, sure. They're okay."

"Good. And your hat, it's satisfactory, too?"

"Keeps the sun off well enough."

"Maybe you don't have any complaints about the company, either. And maybe watching owls is not such a bad way to pass the time."

"You're right on every count, Professor," Nick said wryly.

She rummaged around in the knapsack and handed him a can of grape juice. "So you're enjoying yourself. That's all I ask."

To Lindy it seemed the morning passed much too quickly. The desert heat was dry, and in its own way almost bracing. Nick leaned back against a boulder, training binoculars on the owls for long, lazy periods of time. Lindy took lots of pictures. When Nick wasn't looking, she snapped a photo of him—a close-up showing his hat pushed back, contentment written on his face as he drowsed with his eyes half-closed. She gazed at him through her viewfinder, impressed at the details a zoom lens could pick out: an engaging mole just below Nick's left ear she'd never noticed before, the bold shadow along his jawline that indicated he was growing a beard. Lindy crept a little closer for another shot, this one from a different angle.

"Don't even think about it," Nick warned, still leaning back with his eyes almost shut. Lindy's finger twitched on the camera's trigger, but she gave up and went back to photographing more amenable subjects like cactus flowers.

Toward noon she began regaling Nick with all her owl stories. "One time I crept right up next to a burrow and looked down it. I didn't see anything at first. But then an owl head came poking around the corner, down there in the tunnel. We stared at each other for a while. Nothing else happened. I didn't need anything else to happen. But an owl can scare you, believe me! Once I thought I heard a rattlesnake right next to me, only I couldn't see it anywhere. That gave me the creeps, all right. I figured it out later. Two little owlets had seen me coming, hopped into their burrow and tried to frighten me away by sounding just like a rattlesnake. I tell you, these birds are smart."

Nick listened thoughtfully. "How long have you been coming out here, Lindy?"

"Over three years now. I discovered the owls right after I came to teach at Chamberlin."

"For some reason I keep picturing you as a kid wandering around this place. What were you like as a kid, Professor? In my mind I see you as a solemn little girl with black pigtails, picking up all sorts of rocks and taking them home until your parents yelled at you to stop."

He wasn't far from the truth, although she'd actually worn her hair in a single braid down her back. "Okay, so now and then my parents went haywire when they found piles of rocks in the bathtub or in the kitchen sink. Or in the refrigerator. But they're the ones who got me started in the first place. When I was six, they took me on a trip to Carlsbad Caverns, and that was it. All those marvelous stalagmites and stalactites! I thought I'd stumbled into some giant underground castle. Well, after that I was hooked on rock formations forever." Lindy sighed happily. "I still go back to the caverns at least once a year. Ever been there?"

"No."

"Goodness." She regarded him with consternation. "I can't imagine life without major caves of some type. You don't know what you're missing."

"Maybe you'll invite me to go there with you one time." His voice was teasing, and Lindy didn't know quite how to respond. She took her caverns very seriously.

"I suppose . . . if you were really interested . . ."

"I'm interested in *you*, Linden Eloise. I'm beginning to understand how you grew up to be a geologist. Not to mention an engineer and a teacher. Tell me more about it." His tone was serious now, and Lindy found this even more disconcerting than his teasing. She wanted to tell him all sorts of things about herself—why, she was practically bubbling over with things to tell him. She couldn't seem to stop talking, that was the most disturbing part.

"Well, you see, Nick, when I was a teenager, I found out about the bizarre things that happen when you build a house or a bridge, and you don't consider what's underneath it. I mean, think about all the different types of sediment there are! It can make your head spin. Look at the Leaning Tower of Pisa, if you don't believe me. Talk about needing a really good geologic engineer! So, anyway, I decided in high school that I wanted to be an engineer. And then I was a teaching assistant in college, and I knew I had to be a teacher, too. It's all tremendously exciting! Sometimes I wake up in the morning and grin to myself, just thinking of the day ahead.''

Lindy was buzzing with excitement right this minute, telling Nick about her life. He seemed to bring out the best of her—her enthusiasm, her joy. Maybe it was the way he was looking at her, as if her joy truly mattered to him. As if he took pleasure in her happiness.

But she hadn't brought him all the way out here to talk about herself. The point was to make him talk about his own life. That was the most important part of Lindy's plan, and she had to do a good job of steering him toward the subject. It would be best not to start him out on an empty stomach, however.

''Time for lunch,'' she announced, bringing food out of the knapsack. Both the peanut butter and the cheese would require the aid of her Swiss army knife, and she delved into her purse for it. Of course, that meant extracting Nick's boots first. She placed them neatly side by side on the ground next to him.

He frowned. ''Imagine that. You just happen to be carrying a pair of men's boots in your purse.''

''Oh, I stock everything. Want to see? Here's a chisel, and a compass. Some streak plates for diagnosing minerals—I'm never without those. And look, here's a bottle of vinegar. I always carry that so I can find out when there's calcite in a rock. Did you know calcite will make vinegar fizz? Just one little drop of vinegar. It's the best fizzle in the world.''

Nick's expression had turned ominous again. ''It's bad enough you trussing me into this combat gear. I draw the line at shoes!''

''Well, if you say so. But if you tried them on, you'd find out they're very comfortable.''

"Forget it."

"Your feet probably don't feel so good in those loafers, not with the kind of walking we did this morning. But it's up to you." Lindy found her knife, and proceeded to spread peanut butter on the crackers.

Nick picked up one of the chukka boots, and for a moment she thought he was going to hurl it into the nearest bush.

"WHEE-whee-whee-whee-whee!" said the sentry owl, bobbing like a butler taking a quick bow. "WHEE-whee-whee-whee-whee."

"I'm surrounded," Nick muttered. "Surrounded by creatures!" He took off his loafer and jammed the boot onto his foot. He scowled at it. Then he put on the other boot and started tying the laces.

"How do they feel?" Lindy asked.

"They're too big. That's right. Too damn big."

"I'm glad they're not too small. And we can always go back and exchange them for another size...later," she added hastily at the look he gave her. "No more shopping today. None at all. Here, have a cracker."

She fed him steadily, trying to distract him from the boots. They both devoured quite a feast: raisins, corn chips, almost the whole box of crackers, the entire package of cheese and two kinds of granola bars. Lindy ended up plying Nick with more grape juice.

"So, Nick," she said at last, taking a deep breath, "tell me the truth. Is Aldridge Aviation really that great? I can't help noticing you're frustrated by a lot of things."

He stretched his legs out and regarded the boots on his feet as if he didn't trust them. "Sure, I get frustrated. Too many business meetings, contractors who don't return my phone calls...mule-headed geologists who complain about my engineering reports. Those are just a few of the aggravations. But I'll get through them all right."

Lindy ignored his sarcasm. "Yes, but why should you *have* to get through the aggravation? Why not make your career into exactly what you want it to be?" She scooted closer so she could look straight at him. "I'm beginning to know you a little better, and this is how it seems to me. You like to fly airplanes, and you like to design them. Those are the two things you really want to do. But instead, Aldridge Aviation is such a big company you have to do all this other junk!"

"I wouldn't exactly call it junk," Nick said in a dry tone. He started unlacing one of his boots. "Maybe Aldridge has gotten a lot bigger than I expected, and a lot more complicated. But I'm half owner of the company. I have independence, and that's what I need." He tugged the bootlace free and dangled it in front of his nose as if inspecting it for defects.

"That kind of lace will last for years and years," Lindy informed him. "Calvin personally guarantees all his shoelaces. Especially the bright green ones, like you have. They're top of the line. But listen. You'd have a lot more freedom if you went into business entirely for yourself, Nick. You could run a smaller company, a simpler one."

He laced up his boot again, extra tight this time. "What's your angle on all this, Professor? Even if I did sell out my share of Aldridge Aviation, it wouldn't solve any of your problems. If I left right now—sure, there'd be a lot of delay, a lot of trouble. Juliet doesn't like the details of building a factory, and it'd take her a while to sort everything out. But she'd do it, and the factory would get built."

Lindy decided maybe it was time to redo the laces on her own boots. She worked at one of the knots. "Forget my problems for right now. Forget Juliet's. I'm talking about *you,* Nick. I have a suspicion that all you really want to do is design and fly airplanes. Haven't you ever thought about it? Being on your own, no partner to bother with. Jarrett Aviation, not Aldridge Aviation." She tried to make the idea very enticing, uttering it in a seductive sort of voice. Unfortunately she only sounded like she had a frog in her throat.

"Tell me one thing. Why the heck are we both sitting here, fiddling with our shoelaces?" Nick asked.

"Because we both like our boots," she replied promptly. "It's a sure sign. If we didn't like them, we wouldn't give a fig about the laces. But you didn't answer my question, Nick."

He stood up, pacing back and forth in the experimental way usually reserved for shoe stores. Then he glanced down at Lindy. "All right, I confess. Sure, I've thought about going it on my own. That's only natural. But after what I did to Juliet, hell, I owe her at least one concession. I'll build this damn factory, if it means that much to her."

Lindy struggled to her feet and followed Nick as he did some more pacing in his boots. "What is it with you and Juliet Aldridge? You're so mysterious about it. I don't understand. What could you have done to her that was so awful?''

Nick turned around. He gazed at Lindy as if about to say something of great portent. She almost held her breath, hoping that at last the mystery of Juliet would be revealed.

A long moment passed. ''WHEE-whee-whee-whee-whee!'' scolded the sentry owl. But still Nick didn't speak. Just when Lindy thought she couldn't bear the suspense any longer, he gave a shrug.

''These boots aren't so bad,'' he said grudgingly. ''Definitely a little on the big side, but I suppose I can live with them.''

''Forget the darn boots!'' Lindy exclaimed.

''After all the trouble you've put me through, I'm supposed to forget the boots? That doesn't make any sense.''

Lindy was ready to pound his chest in frustration. ''Nick, if you don't tell me about you and Juliet... Well, you'd better tell me, that's all. I have to know what happened. I just have to know.''

He hesitated another long moment. And then he lifted both hands as if in defeat. ''Okay, okay. Here goes, then—the whole truth about Juliet and me.''

CHAPTER EIGHT

"I LEFT JULIET at the altar. That was my crime, and I've been paying for it ever since."

Nick sat down, reclining against his boulder once more. Lindy continued to pace, hands tucked into the pockets of her khaki pants.

"Goodness. You were going to marry Juliet?"

"That was the idea. It was more *her* idea, but I went along with it for a little while."

Lindy couldn't seem to stand still. Back and forth she went, scuffing her boots in the dirt. She was plagued by jealousy. Motion appeared to be the only answer—as if, by walking fast enough, she could outdistance any unwanted emotion.

"What's she like? Is she pretty?" Lindy knew she was only tormenting herself further, but she needed to understand what kind of woman could get Nick to the altar—if even for a moment.

Nick rubbed the hint of beard along his jaw. "Heck, she looks like . . . a regular person. Red hair. She does that curly stuff to it. And brown eyes. I guess she's pretty. Yeah, sure, she's pretty."

Lindy decided this was enough of a description. Already she could imagine Juliet much too vividly: a sprite of a woman, auburn curls cascading to her shoulders. A woman who loved to fly, who shared Nick's passion for airplanes.

Lindy sat abruptly on the ground. Pacing wasn't helping her anymore. "You didn't marry her," she stated. "That's one thing. At least you didn't marry Juliet."

"It would've been a mistake, only she didn't see it that way. We were friends, right from the first time we met. That's the way things should have stayed."

Lindy picked up a twig that had fallen from the juniper tree. She brushed it over the dirt, sketching a pattern. At least Nick didn't seem to have any romantic notions about Juliet.

"I can't help being curious," Lindy said. "If you only wanted to be friends . . . well, how did you get as far as the altar with her?"

Nick looked disgruntled. "It wasn't exactly something I planned. Juliet and I flew to Las Vegas on a business trip. We were sitting in a bar that night, having a nice casual drink, when all of a sudden she began talking marriage. Just like that—she wanted us to get married. I told her all the reasons it wouldn't work. But then I started thinking . . . why not? We'd been partners on the job six, seven years. Why not have a new kind of partnership? That's what I thought, anyway. By then maybe it was the beer talking." Nick took off his hat and wiped his forehead, as if reliving his narrow escape was proving to be too harrowing. But Lindy had to know all of it.

"What happened next?" she prodded.

"Dammit, what do the details matter?"

Lindy waited. Nick grimaced, but at last he went on, "Okay. So we go down the street to this place called the Happy Blossom Wedding Chapel, and some guy dressed like a toreador is all set to marry us. We get as far as the part where I'm supposed to say 'I do.' Instead I say 'Hell, no' and walk out. Left Juliet standing all by herself with the toreador. End of story.''

Lindy gave a deep sigh of relief. ''Thank goodness. No one can blame you for what you did. It was the only sensible thing.''

Nick pushed a hand through his hair, making it stand up in odd clumps. ''Yeah, well, I let things go too far— I never should've walked up to that altar with her.''

Lindy glanced down at what she'd sketched in the dirt with her twig. Her own personal portrait of Juliet Aldridge: heart-shaped face, big eyes, flowing curls. Of course, Lindy wasn't the most adept artist in the world, and dirt certainly wasn't her medium. Anyone else would think she'd drawn a bug-eyed potato that was beginning to sprout squiggly roots on top. But Lindy could look down at her sketch and see beautiful Juliet, clear as anything.

Lindy slapped her hand on the ground and hastily obliterated the portrait. ''Nick, everything makes sense now. Obviously you can't be partners with Juliet anymore, and you've been thinking about going into business for yourself. So why not just do it?''

He gave her a suspicious glance. ''I don't see how any of this would help your owls. Because that's the only thing on your mind. These damn owls. You're not discussing my career out of simple concern for my welfare.''

She leaned toward him. ''I'm proposing something that would benefit you *and* the owls. What could be better? Today you've seen how wonderful they are, how much they need to be protected. The way I figure it, nothing's stopping you from coming over to my side. First off, you could change the location of the factory. Then, once the owls are safe, you could sell your shares of Aldridge Aviation and start up your own small company and be very satisfied with life.''

Nick stood and began tramping up and down the foxhole, like a prisoner trying to get exercise in a jail cell. The sentry owl watched him without twitching so much as a feather, yellow eyes impassive.

''You had it all figured out today, didn't you?'' Nick said after a moment. ''Bringing me here, working on me. I guess you thought it would be great to solve my career problems and rescue your owls all in one fell swoop. Pretty impressive logic, I'll admit that much.''

Lindy scrambled up and headed Nick off, blocking his path. ''I *do* have good logic. Because I know you want to leave Aldridge. You've said so yourself.''

''First I have a job to finish. Juliet wants this factory built. It's the one last thing I can do for her—and I'm going to do it the best way possible.''

''Look around you,'' Lindy said urgently. ''Really look, for once! How can you allow all this to be destroyed? Oh, if only you'd see it the way I do. Nick, we're visitors here, nothing more. This land belongs to the owls. And to the lizards and the snakes and the spiders. Not to us!''

Nick didn't answer, and she wondered if he'd even heard her. He stared off into the distance with frowning abstraction, his safari hat pushed back on his head. Lindy turned and gazed out over the mesa. It was a wild, untouched landscape. She found it easy to imagine how this place had looked some four hundred years ago, when it was first sighted by the Spaniards. So little had changed. This land and all its creatures had resisted human encroachment for centuries. Until now. Until Aldridge Aviation.

At last Nick spoke, his voice rough in the thin desert air. "Believe it or not, I can see what's here, Lindy. Maybe even the way you want me to see it."

"You mean, you understand how I feel about the owls?"

"Yes, dammit. I'm not saying that changes anything. I still have a factory to build. I'm just saying, heck, this doesn't make any sense. But after being here with you... I'm glad somebody's willing to defend these owls. Somebody like you." He put his hands on her waist and brought her toward him. "It sure doesn't make any sense," he repeated, frowning at her. "But when I look at you—when I touch you—I seem to forget about everything else. Everything reasonable. It's a real problem."

His hands were warm on her, making her feel oddly unsteady. But she felt lighthearted, too. Nick was changing! He hadn't given in yet; he was as stubborn as ever. But he was changing, and that was all she needed for now.

She gazed at him. He looked disgusted with both himself and Lindy. Tortured, in fact. And Lindy could no longer resist him at all. She tossed her cap onto the ground, shaking her hair loose. Nick's hat had to go, too. She reached up, and a second later the safari hat landed in the dirt beside the battered baseball cap. Next Lindy put a hand on either side of Nick's face, savoring the wonderful scratchiness of his beard. Then she brought his face down to hers and kissed him.

She was eager and impatient, bumping noses with him a few times before she got the hang of what she was doing. But he helped. He helped a lot, his hands tangling in her hair, cradling her head, bringing her still closer. She sighed against his mouth, knowing she wasn't ever going to let go of him. She'd kiss him forever here in her foxhole, whether or not the sentry owl approved. Nothing mattered but Nick.

Lindy thought she'd known joy before. But she hadn't. Joy was the passion Nick gave her, the way his body strained to hers. Joy was believing he had captured the magic of the mesa for himself and was sharing it with her. She moved her hands along his shoulders and let her fingers twine in his silky hair. Of course, his hair was so short that twining was a little difficult. But she managed it.

A low humming filled the air, far away yet persistent. Gradually it grew louder. Lindy stirred reluctantly in Nick's arms. "What can that be?" she whispered.

"Who cares? It'll go away." His mouth descended on hers again and she gave in willingly to his power. For she had her own sweet power—she could feel Nick trembling to her touch. "Lindy," he murmured, his voice husky. "Lindy, come here. Come closer..."

She didn't know how she could mold herself any closer to him; he was already holding her so tightly she could scarcely breathe. But she did her best to comply by wrapping her arms fiercely around his neck. And by kissing him again...

The humming in the air intensified, as if the wild pulsing of blood through Lindy's veins was being magnified a thousand times. But this was an intrusion that could no longer be ignored. Lindy broke away from Nick and shaded her eyes to stare into the sky. A helicopter was descending, ominous as a hawk swooping down for the kill. Every owl vanished into its burrow, even the sentry diving for cover. The helicopter brought its own storm along, its rotor churning the breeze into a miniature tornado. Lindy dashed to rescue her baseball cap and Nick's safari hat before they could swirl away like two tumbleweeds.

The helicopter settled onto the mesa with a slight rocking motion, reminding Lindy of some immense, ponderous bird with feet too big for a graceful landing. "What's going on?" she shouted at Nick over the roar of that blasted rotor. He answered, but she couldn't make out the words. His shrug indicated he was as puzzled as she.

Lindy hadn't wanted to leave his embrace, not when she was just discovering the delight of it. She felt bereft. She stood with her arms hugged against her body, hair whipping into her face. And now someone was climbing out of the helicopter, bending down to run toward Nick. It was a woman with frizzy, bright red hair.

Once clear of the helicopter, the woman straightened up and waved exuberantly to Nick. She was very tall, a big solid person, yet she moved with surprising speed and delicacy. Lindy had seen football players who could run like that: broad shoulders held still, muscular legs sprinting effortlessly down the field.

Muscular legs and all, this woman possessed curves that could only be called astounding. She displayed them well in a skintight, black lamé jumpsuit that shimmered in the sun. And she jiggled in a most impressive manner as she loped toward Nick. Now she waved both hands, calling excitedly to him. Lindy watched as the woman flung herself into Nick's arms, as jubilant as Hammersmith when he greeted someone.

The woman was so big it was a wonder she didn't slam Nick right to the ground. Once again Lindy thought of football players going in for the tackle. Nick remained upright somehow, but his face wore a look of shock. After a moment the redhead stepped back and started talking to him at a good clip, gesturing expansively. Nick pantomimed, too, pointing at his ears and shaking his head. The woman laughed. She grabbed hold of his arm, and together they began walking quickly across the mesa. Away from Lindy.

No chance! Lindy hurried after them, although she felt absurdly like a tagalong. The roar of the helicopter seemed to be locking her out of the scene, as if she were watching Nick and this woman through a closed window. At last they were all far enough away from the darn helicopter for a conversation to take place. Unfortunately the conversation was two-sided, between Nick and his large, exuberant lady friend. Neither one of them seemed aware of Lindy hovering beside them.

"Romeo, Romeo!" exclaimed the woman in a rich contralto voice. "Damn, but it's good to see you."

Nick scowled. "Juliet, I keep asking you not to call me that."

"But you *are* my own true Romeo. You know you are. And I'm your Juliet." She tucked her hand companionably in the crook of his arm. Then she leaned closer to him, murmuring low in his ear as if well aware of Lindy's presence, after all, and seeking privacy. Lindy caught a word here and there, but she didn't try to listen. She was more interested in Juliet's appearance than anything else.

She still couldn't believe this was Juliet Aldridge, here in all her stunning flesh. The woman was so completely different from the slender, auburn-haired nymph Lindy had envisioned. She was every bit as tall as Nick. And she wasn't beautiful, not by any stretch of the imagination. Her bright red hair looked as if it had seen one too many perms and her face was as round as a pie tin. Even so, she was a dazzling woman. Absolutely dazzling. Her body had something to do with it: the startling combination of height and muscle and feminine curves. But that wasn't all. Juliet Aldridge shone and sparkled with some inner source of liveliness. It bubbled out of her now in a throaty laugh, interspersing her stream of talk to Nick. Lindy suddenly felt too quiet and simple, like a lump of plain old pipe clay eclipsed by the fiery color of a gypsum desert rose.

"Slow down, Juliet," Nick ordered at last. "You can't just whistle your way in here and start telling me a bunch of company gossip like I only saw you yesterday. What the heck are you doing in New Mexico?"

Juliet widened her eyes in an expression obviously meant to be guileless. All it did was make her cheeks rounder. "I thought I'd check in with you. See how the project was going, look at this factory site for my-self. There's nothing unusual about that.''

Nick was obviously skeptical. ''In St. Louis you said you weren't interested in the day-to-day details of this project. Why the sudden change?''

''Don't get bent out of shape. It's a good thing I did come out here. Look at your hair! What did you do to it? Looks like someone went after you with a buzz saw.''

He rubbed the back of his neck. ''I don't want to hear any more about this confounded haircut. You got that? Forget the haircut. Erase the damn haircut from your brain!''

''Well, I'll be, Romeo. You're a mite testy today. But I have some news that'll make you happy. I brought Ray Silverstein with me from St. Louis. We chartered the copter in Albuquerque, and now he's waiting in it to talk to you.''

Nick became all business. ''That's good. It's great, in fact. I was going to call him tomorrow, but it's bet-ter he's here. I need to ask him how he's coming with those changes on the building specs.'' With that Nick strode off toward the helicopter.

Lindy opened her mouth to protest, but she never got a word out. Juliet grabbed her hand and shook it forcefully. ''Hello, MacAllister. It's about time you and I met. We have a lot to talk about.'' She smiled at Lindy with no apparent malice. She possessed the kind of smile that could only be called a grin. It was wide and confident, making no effort to disguise strong, white, too-large teeth. Big teeth, frizzy hair, round cheeks... How could this odd combination of features be so attractive? And, blast it, how did the wretched woman know who Lindy was? She probably had spies running around everywhere!

"Hello," Lindy said stiffly. "As a matter of fact, Ms. Aldridge, I do have a lot to talk to you about—"

"Call me Juliet. First off, let's discuss this kissing thing I saw from the air. How serious is it between you and Nick?"

Lindy was so unprepared for Juliet's question that she actually tried to answer it. "What you saw—Nick and I—we were—" She stopped, flummoxed.

Juliet nodded slowly. "I'm getting the picture. It's serious, but not as bad as I thought. You see, Linden, I can tell you have a hankering for Nick, but you don't want to admit that yet. Once you *do* admit it, you'll be somebody to contend with. Until that happens, I'm not too worried about you."

Lindy flushed, angry and embarrassed. What could Juliet Aldridge possibly know about her feelings? Especially when Lindy was thoroughly confused about them herself!

Juliet was smiling. She looked sly and merry, like an overgrown elf who knew any number of secrets about Lindy and Nick—secrets she wouldn't hesitate to use to her own advantage. Lindy was fed up. Juliet Aldridge had been doing everything possible to make her feel off balance and unsure of herself. Maybe that strategy had succeeded for a few moments, but Lindy wasn't going to put up with it any longer.

"Ms. Aldridge, you'll have to play your games with someone else. My only business with you is the factory site."

Juliet looked offended. "I don't play games, as you put it. And forget the factory. We're talking about Nick right now. Bottom line is, I want him. I'll do anything I can to get him. I'm giving you fair warning, and I don't see how you can complain about *that*."

Juliet Aldridge was a disconcerting woman, no doubt about it. Once again Lindy was taken by surprise. She couldn't think of a single retort, a single argument. The helicopter went on buzzing in the distance like a pesky insect. At last Nick came jogging away from it. He reached Juliet and spoke to her.

"Ray's all ready to work on the blueprints. And I've decided to send him on to California after we're done— I want him to run that inspection at the Meridian plant."

Juliet beamed. "That's a wonderful idea. Ray and I have already booked rooms at a hotel in town. The three of us can work there."

"Fine. I don't want to waste any time since he's going to California. Let's get started."

Lindy stood very still. "Nick, we have an agreement, remember? You can't just leave in the middle of things!"

"Lord, I almost forgot about that cockeyed deal I made with you. But how was I supposed to know something like this would come up? You'll have to give me some leeway."

"We made a deal," Lindy said stubbornly. "That's all there is to it. No excuses allowed for either one of us."

Juliet was listening with obvious interest. "Exactly what kind of agreement is this? I want to know all about it."

Neither Lindy nor Nick answered her. They simply stared at each other in a silent battle of wills. Then Nick drew Lindy away from Juliet a few yards.

"Look," he said in a low, harsh voice. "It's very important for me to work with Silverstein right now. You and I—we'll make some other arrangement later. I'm being reasonable about this. Why can't you be the same way?"

Lindy glared at him. She clenched her teeth so hard it hurt. Only with a conscious effort could she relax her jaw enough to speak. "You're not supposed to do any business until the engineering report is filed. There's no way to compromise on that."

"Right, Professor. How could I forget? You never compromise on anything, do you?" His tone was mocking.

"Twenty-four hours. That's what you promised me." She was appalled to find her voice shaking, and she struggled to control it. "How can you go back on your promise? And all because of Juliet!"

"Did I hear my name?" Juliet called in a throaty trill. "I really don't think you should talk about me unless I'm in on it."

The woman probably had radar installed in her ears. Lindy dragged Nick another few yards away.

"You know she contrived this whole thing," Lindy whispered fiercely. "It's all a setup. Her spies probably told her you were spending too much time with me, so she decided to do something about it. Don't you think it's interesting how she just happened to show up in a helicopter while we're out here? This is no coincidence.''

"Now you're being paranoid."

Frustrated, Lindy smacked her baseball cap against the safari hat. "Why won't you listen to me? You said yourself she wasn't interested in the details of this project. But suddenly she's here. Something's fishy and you know it."

Nick's expression was implacable, unyielding. "Juliet is perfectly capable of hatching a harebrained plot. And maybe that's what she did this time. But I don't know, and I don't care. Because I still need to talk to Silverstein right away. You and I can finish our business later."

Lindy wanted to plead with him. She wanted to remind him that he'd kissed her passionately just a short while ago. Hadn't that meant anything to him? But she was too proud to ask the question aloud, especially when Juliet was watching.

"Please," was all Lindy whispered. "Don't go with her. Stay with me."

Nick swore under his breath. "I know what you're doing. You're turning this into some distorted test of loyalty. If I go with Juliet, I'm a traitor. If I stay here with you, I'm a good guy, and I get to wear a white hat. That's it, isn't it?"

Lindy didn't say anything. She glanced down at the dark green safari hat she was holding. *That* was the hat she wanted Nick to wear, blast it. But he didn't seem interested in it anymore. Slowly she raised her head and looked at him, waiting for him to make his decision.

His eyes were cold blue now, icy as a mountain stream in winter. "I'm only going to say this one more time, Lindy. I'm not Donald Cluny. I don't hurt people, and I don't betray them. I'll give you the rest of your twenty-four hours, but first I'm going to talk to Silverstein. Read whatever you want into that. If you don't trust me—hell, there's nothing I can do about it."

He walked back to Juliet and said something to her. Juliet listened, then gave an exultant laugh. She waved at Lindy.

"Better luck next time!" she called. "So long, Linden MacAllister." With that she and Nick started toward the helicopter. They both moved with long, easy strides, as if well accustomed to each other's rhythm. Nick didn't turn around even once to glance at Lindy. His camouflaged back receded from her inexorably. Juliet, however, turned and waved two more times, cheerful as anything. In her black jumpsuit, she looked like a deep-sea diver who had risen, glittering, from the sea. She made a bizarre yet striking impression; not a woman any man could easily forget. And when she tucked her hand once more into the crook of Nick's arm, he didn't move away from her.

The two of them climbed into the helicopter, and a moment later it lifted into the sky with a high-pitched whine of its rotor. Lindy shaded her eyes and watched it go. She stood alone on the mesa, feeling numb inside—as empty as some cavern left forgotten deep in the earth. Nick had gone. That was all she knew— Nick had gone.

CHAPTER NINE

THE SENTRY OWL emerged cautiously from his burrow. At first only his head was visible, looking rather like a dumpling in a bowl of soup. Gradually he grew bolder, coming to perch on the very top of his mound. His slender legs were angled apart in a defiant stance, as if he was daring any helicopter to swoop down on him from the sky again.

"Don't worry. The darn thing's gone," Lindy told him from her foxhole. "It's just you and me."

He gazed at her solemnly, then swiveled his head left and right as if he didn't believe her. Lindy sat with her arms wrapped tightly around her knees. In the past she'd spent countless hours alone with her owls, yet she'd never been lonely. Bringing Nick here had changed all that. Right now she felt a loneliness so immense, so heavy, she feared she might crack under its weight like a brittle eggshell. She leaned her forehead against her knees and closed her eyes.

"Blast you, Nick Jarrett! It's not fair. None of it is fair." She'd been so sure he was changing, starting to see her point of view. He'd even begun settling into his camouflage clothes. He'd kissed her as the Cluny never had—with a wild, sweet desire. But then Juliet had appeared out of the sky, and he'd reverted. Once again he'd become the powerful executive from Al-

dridge Aviation who was going to destroy this place.
He and Juliet made a wonderful pair, both of them tall
and strong and ruthless. Maybe they really belonged
together, and some day they'd end up back at the
Happy Blossom Wedding Chapel. Well, that was none
of Lindy's concern. She would fight both of them with
everything she had. She'd protect her owls. And afterward, when it was all over—when she'd won the
battle—Nick and Juliet could go off somewhere together and do whatever they pleased.

She lifted her head and gazed at the sentry owl. He
seemed to be regarding her with a skeptical expression. She pushed the tangled hair back from her face,
a new and very unwelcome thought coming to her.

"Oh, no," she told the owl. "Don't look at me like
that. If you think I'm falling in love with Nick Jarrett, you're very mistaken. I'm angry at him, maybe
even a little hurt. A lot hurt. But I'm not in love with
him!"

The owl's yellow eyes remained unblinking. Lindy
scrambled to her feet and hurriedly began repacking
her knapsack. The whirlwind whipped up by the helicopter had scattered the remains of her meal with
Nick. The empty corn-chip bag was plastered against
a bush, and the flimsy boxes of raisins and crackers
had gone helter-skelter over the ground. Lindy scrab-
bled here and there, retrieving everything she could. It
had been such a good picnic lunch—a happy one. Now
there was nothing left but this pathetic trash to be
gathered, and Lindy kept expecting to see one of Juliet's spies lurking behind the juniper tree.

Finally there was only one thing left to pack: Nick's
safari hat. Lindy shook it by the brim. Then she gave

the crown a punch with her fist. But it was a sturdy hat, and none of her abuse did any damage. Lindy stuffed it into the knapsack. She swung her purse over one shoulder, her camera and binoculars over the other. Beginning the trek to her car, she left the factory site behind. The sentry owl sent an echo after her: "WHEE-whee-whee-whee-whee." He sounded mournful, as if he realized his home was doomed. And he sounded as if he knew Lindy was in danger, too— in terrible danger of loving Nick Jarrett.

LINDY WAS WEARING her comfort clothes. These were clothes she dug out of her closet only when she was feeling very blue or distressed. She'd never needed them as much as she did tonight. She huddled on her sofa in full attire: a faded T-shirt with a hole under one arm, a patchwork sweater with sleeves that were too long, jeans that were wearing out in the seat and the knees, thick, striped socks that went halfway up her legs.

On the coffee table beside her was a selection of her best rocks, including her favorite piece of oyster limestone. And she was cradling a half-eaten bowl of triple-fudge-banana-swirl frozen yogurt. Hammersmith was curled up on the sofa with her, his nose pointing hopefully at the bowl. Lindy stroked his floppy yellow ears and tried for the hundredth time not to think about Nick. Was he with Juliet right now? Perhaps they were sharing a late, intimate dinner somewhere. Lindy huddled deeper in her sweater and took another mouthful of triple-fudge-banana-swirl. Hammersmith wagged his tail and panted on her. She was surrounded by warm, cozy dog breath. Yet she still felt rotten.

The doorbell sounded, and immediately pandemonium ensued on the sofa. Lindy and Hammersmith fought to disentangle themselves. The bowl of frozen yogurt landed on the floor—right-side up, fortunately. Hammersmith bounded off the sofa and went slurping after the bowl. Again the doorbell sounded its imperious demand.

"I'm coming. Hold on to your turnips," Lindy grumbled. She padded to the door and looked out the peephole. She wasn't at all pleased with what she saw.

"What are *you* doing here?" she demanded as she swept the door open. "It's almost midnight."

"I'd hoped for a better welcome than that, Linden. I have something to say that you're going to find very interesting. Extremely interesting, as a matter of fact." Juliet Aldridge came charging into the house without waiting for an invitation. She made a slap-slap-slap sound that Lindy couldn't identify at first. Then she noticed Juliet was wearing rubber thongs that flapped against her feet with every step. Each of her toenails was painted a different color. Cherry-red, pink, apricot, magenta—an artist's entire palette.

"Why, this is some place you have here. I love these old adobe houses, I really do. And look at this—my kind of dog." Juliet didn't seem phased in the least when Hammersmith catapulted toward her. She allowed him to give her several enthusiastic licks as she patted his fuzzy head. "My, what a cute little puppy you are," she crooned. "Itsy-bitsy little puppy dog, that's you. Teensiest puppy dog there ever was! Give us another big kiss now."

Lindy winced, but Hammersmith seemed ecstatic to have someone talk silly to him. He pranced beside Juliet as she slapped into the living room. She sat down, her large body seeming to consume the entire sofa. Propping her feet on the coffee table, she grinned at Lindy.

"Well, don't you want to hear what I have to say?"

Lindy stood in the arched doorway to the room and folded her arms. She was seething. In the space of about five seconds flat, Juliet Aldridge had taken over her house, her sofa and her dog. Juliet seemed to add a new source of light to the room, dressed as she was in a pair of bright orange romper shorts. Her slinky halter top displayed all her curves and muscles to best effect. Once again Lindy felt eclipsed by this woman — dowdy in her old jeans and shapeless sweater.

"All right. If you really have something to say, talk. Hammers, come over here, boy. Hammers...come *here*."

Hammersmith wagged his floppy tail, but he stayed right where he was beside the sofa, staring up at Juliet with an expression of complete adoration. Lindy marched over to him and started pushing him by the rear end toward her easy chair. His nails screeched in protest over the wooden floor, and he turned to gaze mournfully at Juliet as the distance between them widened. Lindy plunked herself down in the limp old cushions of her chair, holding on to Hammersmith's collar. He squirmed, and she had to keep a firm grip so he wouldn't go bounding back to Juliet. It was humiliating, this betrayal by her own dog! Juliet, however, seemed immensely pleased. She grinned wider, showing her large teeth.

"Wouldn't mind a dog like that myself. Are you willing to sell him?"

"No!" Lindy tightened her grip still further on Hammersmith's collar.

"Just asking." Juliet glanced around the living room, perhaps looking for something else she might purchase. "This place reminds me of the house I grew up in. Lots and lots of books scattered about, nothing very orderly or neat. I had four big brothers, and you could never keep a place neat with those guys. Always left their hockey equipment where you'd be most likely to trip over it." Juliet gave a throaty chuckle.

Lindy reached over to the coffee table with her free hand and grabbed the pair of gardening gloves Hammersmith had chewed into shreds. She stuffed their remains into a pottery bowl, but there wasn't much else she could do about the disorder in the room—the stacks of nature magazines she could never bear to throw out, the geologic survey maps tied into bundles or taped haphazardly to the walls, the piles of rocks she hadn't sorted yet.

She looked impatiently at Juliet. "Is this why you came here in the middle of the night? To let me know my house is messy and to tell me the story of your childhood?"

"My life story *is* very instructive." Juliet examined her feet as if trying to decide which toenail she liked best. "You see, Linden, with all those big brothers, I had to learn early on how to speak up and get what I wanted out of life. I learned how to race to the fridge ahead of my brothers. How to beat them at hockey, and how to make their friends ask me out on dates."

Juliet laughed again, obviously delighted with herself. "You know what? I'm still working at it—learning exactly how to achieve what I want. Why else do you think I came to New Mexico just now? When one of my representatives out here faxed a photo to me— a photo of you and Nick together—well, I knew it was time to act."

Lindy stroked Hammersmith's ears. "Go on," she said sharply. "Only I don't want to hear about you and your disgusting spies. Let's get to the point."

Juliet stretched her long, muscular legs. Lindy would have expected athletic legs like that to be deeply tanned. Instead, they were as white as two ivory pillars come to life. It was disconcerting. But then, everything about the woman was disconcerting.

"You said you think I'm playing some kind of game, didn't you, Linden? But I'm not. I believe in being absolutely straightforward. That's how I get what I want—whether it's from my brothers or someone like you. So, here it is. I have a proposition for you. I'll give up the location of the factory. I'll build somewhere else and let you have all those owl burrows to yourself. On one condition, of course. You have to give up something in return. Namely, Nick Jarrett."

Lindy was stunned by this proposal, and let go of Hammersmith's collar. But Hammers stayed where he was, apparently content to adore Juliet from afar.

"You must be joking!" Lindy exclaimed after a moment. "You can't bargain for a man the way you would for a . . . a sack of peanuts. But even if I agreed to something this preposterous, what makes you think Nick will have you? He's a very strong-willed person, and he won't do something just because *you* want him to."

Juliet's face looked a little less round and cheerful all of a sudden, as if someone had pinched her cheeks. "I suppose he told you about the Happy Blossom incident. I was afraid of that. It's a good thing I'm intervening when I am. Nick wouldn't have told you about the Happy Blossom unless he was starting to get serious about you and thought he had to explain himself. But I'm the one who's right for him, and once you're out of the way he'll soon come to realize it. You leave all that to me."

Lindy picked up her dessert bowl, now thoroughly clean after Hammersmith's tongue had done its work. She thumped the bowl down on the coffee table, within an inch of Juliet's variegated toenails. "I've discovered one thing. I respect Nick Jarrett, no matter how much I disagree with him about the factory. He's a man of integrity. He won't go for any of your schemes! He'll make his own choices, for the reasons *he* thinks are right."

Juliet flashed her wide, exuberant grin. "If I change my mind about building this factory, Nick will actually be relieved. At this very minute he's still at the hotel with Ray, talking about the possibility of expanding our California plant. That's what he really wants us to do. And he'll never know about my little conversation with you tonight. You're certainly not going to tell him, Linden."

"I won't be part of this—"

"Sure, you will. Because I've made you an offer you can't refuse. This is your one and only chance to save those owls. You couldn't live with yourself if you picked Nick, instead. So I get rid of my competition, just like that. Did I come up with a good plan or what? Sometimes I amaze even myself."

Lindy stared at her. "I still don't believe this. I thought the factory was so important to you."

"Nick is more important." Juliet's voice was almost soft. "He and I...we've been partners, we've been friends. Only that's not enough anymore. You see, Linden, I'm not like you—I'm honest about my feelings. I want Nick. Hang it, I love the guy. If only he'd stayed with me at the Happy Blossom...But I'll get another chance with him. That's all there is to it." Juliet sounded defiant. She stood up and slap-slapped her way to the front door, frizzy red hair sailing out behind her. Then she turned and gazed at Lindy.

"So, what's your answer? It's going to be a whole lot of trouble giving up that factory site. But I'm willing to go ahead—as long as you agree to my terms."

Lindy struggled up from the sagging cushions of the easy chair. She came to face Juliet, Hammersmith right on her heels. "You say you're such a straightforward person. But you're not at all! You sneak around, hiring spies and trying to manipulate people. I bet you don't even have four brothers. That's probably just a story you toss out when it's convenient. I don't trust you one bit."

By now Juliet was merry again, looking like a big, mischievous kid in her romper outfit. "Believe it or not, I do have all those brothers. Two of them are single, by the way, and I'd be glad to introduce you to them. Well! I'm off. I'll give you some time to think about your answer, but you'd better make up your mind soon. This is a limited offer. Bye, doggie. Itsy-bitsy cutie pie!''

Hammersmith started galloping after Juliet as she went down the walk. Lindy grabbed him just in time, throwing her arms around his middle. Together they skidded in a tumble against the door, slamming it shut. Hammersmith was not one to hold a grudge, however. As Lindy sat down hard on the floor, he licked her face with enthusiasm. Then he flopped down next to her, putting his head in her lap as if he'd forgotten all about the likes of Juliet Aldridge.

Lindy wanted to forget about Juliet, too, but it was impossible. She leaned back against the door, feeling as limp and worn as the cushions of her chair. What on earth was she going to do now? Juliet's proposal was absurd, demeaning, sickening—but it would rescue the owls. Wasn't that the one thing Lindy had wanted all along?

She stayed where she was for some time, patting Hammersmith's forehead distractedly. It was painful to imagine her life without Nick. Never again to see him, never again to know his touch or his kiss...

She could no longer deny the truth Juliet had pointed out to her. She was falling in love with Nick, and she didn't know how to stop herself. Juliet had presented her with an impossible choice! It would tear Lindy apart to relinquish Nick. It would also tear her apart to abandon her owls. She despised Juliet for what she was doing. She'd never despised anyone quite like this before, not even the Cluny after his betrayal.

Some strong, clattering noises could be heard outside. Then the doorbell pealed again. Lindy twisted around, unceremoniously dumping Hammersmith's head from her lap. She didn't even bother to stand up. Kneeling awkwardly, she yanked open the door.

"Darn it, Juliet Aldridge, just get the heck away from my house—" She stopped hollering when she realized she was staring at a pair of camouflaged legs. And at two feet in brand-new chukka boots.

Lindy scooted backward, trying to close the door before Nick could come inside. But Hammersmith had taken matters into his own paws. He leapt joyously at Nick, crowding the doorway so Lindy didn't have any room to maneuver. Nick worked his way inside inch by inch, trying to fend off Hammers.

"You forgot about those boulders you left at my place, Professor. But I brought them back to you, mica and all. Only trouble is, I dropped one on my way through your garden. Some of your flowers might look a little flat from now on— Down, you hairy mutt! All right, that's it, that's enough. *Sit!*"

Amazingly, Hammers did exactly as he was told. He sat down in a perfect pose of obedience, although he did give Nick a reproachful stare.

"How'd you get him to do that?" Lindy asked, her voice coming out in an odd croak.

Nick glanced suspiciously at Hammers. "I guess I have that special air of authority. But what are you doing on the floor?"

"Nothing. Please go. I have to... I have to think, and I can't do it if you're here."

He ignored her request, clasping both her hands in his and drawing her up to stand beside him. "What's been going on, Professor? Why'd you start yelling about Juliet?"

"No reason." Lindy pulled away.

"Was she here? What did she say to you?"

"Just go! Please." Lindy was shivering in the night air, even though it wasn't cold.

Nick closed the front door and shot the bolt home. "I'm not going anywhere. I promised you twenty-four hours, and that's what you're going to get. So far we've done maybe five hours. That means we have nineteen more ahead of us. I'm not leaving until they're up." He checked his watch.

This situation was getting worse by the minute. Lindy padded into the living room, her striped socks whispering over the wooden floor. "I won't hold you to that twenty-four hours, Nick. Things have changed since we made our deal. Go away. I'll never be able to think all this through if you're around!"

Nick reached her in a few strides and took her by the shoulders. He regarded her intently. "I want to hear everything. Talk, Professor. Spill it. Speak!"

Hammersmith barked from his sitting position in the hall. He wagged his tail energetically, but Nick shook his head.

"Not you, mutt. I'm still waiting, Lindy."

She nudged a toe at one of her geologic maps that had rolled onto the floor. "Juliet *was* here. But what we discussed is private."

"I don't like the sound of this. I don't like it one bit."

Hammersmith whimpered from the hallway, and Lindy was glad to have her attention distracted from Nick.

"Come here, boy. You don't need to go on sitting there anymore."

Hammersmith wagged his tail frantically, but he didn't budge.

"Here, boy. Come on!"

He whimpered again, as if he longed with all his heart to jump up and run to Lindy. But he stayed right where he was. Lindy coaxed him again and again to come to her, using every inducement she knew. She brought a dog biscuit from the kitchen and held it out to him, waving it back and forth a few feet from his nose. Even that didn't work.

She turned to Nick. "Now look what you've done. This is terrible. Hammers can't move!"

"Hey, it's not my fault. I told him to sit, that's all."

"And he's sitting. He can't do anything else. Are you happy?"

Nick rubbed his jaw, where his beard was already coming in darker and thicker. "It doesn't make any sense. Has the dog ever done this before?"

"No. He *never* does what anybody tells him. This is the first time, and I find it very disturbing."

"Come here, mutt," Nick ordered. "Heel! Roll over. Play dead."

None of these commands had any effect. After some experimenting, it appeared that Hammersmith answered only to "sit" and "speak." And he spoke a lot, whining and groaning his despair.

"Why don't we just move him ourselves?" Nick asked. "I'll pick up one end, you handle the other."

"No, we can't do that. Hammers is obviously in a great deal of psychological distress, and we don't want to make it any worse. You told him to sit, he believes he has to sit. Until we find the key to release him, he'll have to go on sitting."

"Lord, do you want to get him a shrink?"

Lindy glared at Nick. "There *are* dog psychologists, you know. Maybe not in Santiago, but they do exist."

"I bet you'd find a few in St. Louis. There's nothing like the convenience of a big city. That's what I always say."

Lindy wondered what would happen next. The way this night was going, she wouldn't have been surprised if the roof caved in. She set some water and a bowl of Hammersmith's favorite dog food in front of him. He didn't even give the food a sniff. Instead he gazed imploringly at Lindy, his big brown eyes looking like they were about to fill with tears.

"I know, boy," she murmured, stroking his ears. "We'll get you out of this somehow. Don't worry."

"I'd say you both need a shrink. Actually, after being around the two of you, I probably need a shrink."

"You're not helping. I think the best thing to do is leave him alone for a few minutes. Maybe then he'll forget about sitting." Lindy strode into the kitchen, followed by Nick. Hammersmith wailed at this desertion, not realizing it was for his own benefit.

Nick glanced around Lindy's kitchen with a puzzled expression. "What are you trying to do? Grow a garden in here?"

"It's been a very good year for rhubarb." And, indeed, there were bunches of rhubarb everywhere—spilling from the dish drain, spread out fan-shaped on the table and counters. The sight of all those rosy stalks with their generous, rippled leaves helped to soothe Lindy just a little. She took a knife and started

whacking leaves off rhubarb stalks. That was soothing, too.

Nick sat down on a stool across the counter and
watched her activities with a frown. She tapped her
knife against the cutting board.

"Nick, do you really intend to sit here and plague
me for nineteen hours?"

"It was your idea in the first place. And if the mutt
can sit, so can I." Nick glanced at his watch. "Make
that eighteen hours, twenty-six minutes and ten seconds."

"Wonderful." Lindy chopped with greater force.
Hammersmith bleated from the hallway. Nick picked
up one of the rhubarb stalks as it went flying off the
cutting board.

"Who'd want to eat something like this? Looks like
a mutant celery stick."

He could scoff all he liked, but rhubarb was inspir-
ing. No doubt about it. Lindy set down her knife and
gazed at him with growing excitement.

"Nick, I know you feel guilty about Juliet and the
Happy Blossom Wedding Chapel. But haven't you already paid enough for that night? Stop feeling guilty,
that's all! And then...join forces with me. If we stand
together, this plot of hers will never work."

He thumped two stalks of rhubarb together as if
they were drumsticks. "What plot? I can tell something rotten is going on. Exactly why did Juliet show
up here tonight?"

Lindy bit her lip. She didn't know how much to tell
him. So much was at stake! She went around the
counter to him and pushed all the rhubarb away.

"Nick, listen. What Juliet said tonight—does it really matter? She'd say anything to get what she wants. All we have to do is stick together against her, and everything will work out. That's the point. You and I were starting to be together this afternoon, on the mesa. I didn't imagine it . . . did I?" Her voice had gone low. Nick reached out and stroked her cheek with one gentle finger.

"I could have spent the entire day out there with you, Lindy. The night, too. No, you didn't imagine anything." He smoothed her hair back from her face and smiled a little. "Even your jewelry is made of rocks. I like that."

Lindy's hands went to the small chunks of garnet she'd fashioned into crude earrings. "I can't help myself. I see a rock, any rock, and I'm a goner."

"Then pretend I'm a rock, Professor." Nick captured her hands and drew her close. He was still sitting on the stool, and his face was almost level with hers. There was no pain left in her, no hurt. Because Nick was going to kiss her again.

Lindy waited for his kiss, and the waiting was so very calm and easy. So very right. Nick went on smiling at her. And when the waiting was quite perfect and complete, he closed his eyes and brought his lips to hers.

Yes, oh yes . . . he kissed her.

CHAPTER TEN

HAMMERSMITH GAVE A YELP—whether of joy or consternation, it was impossible to tell. But he bounded into the kitchen and hurled himself at Nick and Lindy, knocking them clean apart. Nick almost tumbled off his stool.

"What the devil?"

"Hammers, you're not sitting anymore. You're cured!"

"I can take care of that," Nick grumbled. "All I have to do is say one little word—"

"No! Whatever you do, not that again. But I think Hammersmith is jealous of you. Isn't that wonderful?"

"Yeah, it's great." Nick gave Hammers a sour look. Hammers wagged his tail and licked Nick's hand, perfectly willing to be friends again.

Lindy was still light-headed from Nick's kiss, and had to sit down on a stool. "You know, we have a lot to talk about," she said happily. "I'm so glad you saw what was really out there on the mesa. You saw the owls the way they should be seen. Surely now you'll change the factory site—because you want to save the owls, not because of anything to do with Juliet. Of course, she won't be any too pleased. You and me fighting this thing together—it won't fit into her schemes at all. She'll try to retaliate, but we can handle that—"

"Slow down." Nick turned from Hammersmith and wiped his hand on his camouflage pants. "Who said anything about changing the factory site? Did you think you could slip that into the conversation and I wouldn't notice?"

"You agreed that we shared something on the mesa. You said I wasn't imagining it. And naturally I assumed—"

"Naturally." Nick's mouth twisted in a mirthless smile. "You're really something, Linden Eloise. What we shared today was personal. Between you and me alone. It didn't have anything to do with the damn factory."

"Yes, it did," she insisted, gripping one of the rhubarb stalks. "Because we started to look at the factory the same way! I know we did."

Nick took a rhubarb stalk and yanked the leaf right off it. "Shouldn't you rephrase that? I started to see things the *right* way. *Your* way."

Anger stirred in her. "Blast it, once and for all I *am* right about this. And unless you can see that, Nick, Juliet will succeed. Whatever you and I could have together, it'll be gone. She'll destroy it."

For a long moment he didn't say anything. They sat facing each other, armed with their rhubarb stalks like two opponents ready for an absurd duel of botanical swords. Hammersmith had settled down between them as if he had full confidence everything would work out in the end. But a cold, heavy feeling was growing inside Lindy, a conviction that things *weren't* going to work out. Not at all.

Nick's face went hard, his tenderness vanished. "Next thing I know, you'll tell me I'm betraying you. You've been waiting for a chance to accuse me of that ever since we met."

"Very well," Lindy said quietly. "Maybe you are betraying me. Because I trusted in your decency, Nick. I trusted you'd see that a few innocent creatures are more important than all the trouble and expense of moving your factory. And you know what else? I trusted you'd stand with me against Juliet Aldridge."

"Stop bringing Juliet into this. You want to blame her for everything. But you're the problem, Lindy. Only you. Right now you're secretly relieved you can be disappointed in me. I'm on the Cluny blacklist for sure—and you can deal with me there. I'm no longer a threat to your safety."

"That's not true! You don't know how I really feel. About you or anything else—"

"I know enough, Professor. You've decided no one's ever going to hurt you again. You might as well build a statue of the Cluny. Memorial to a traitor—that's what you could call it. Just to make sure you never forget what he did. And to make sure no other man gets too close to you." Nick tossed down his stalk of rhubarb in a gesture of contempt. He stood and walked out of the room without giving Lindy another glance.

Hammers stayed beside her, pressed right up against her leg. Perhaps he realized she needed his support. Her anger at Nick's injustice was as hot and searing as a lava flow. He was wrong about her! She was ready to give so much to him, ready to allow him into her heart. Nick was the one who wouldn't let her get close.

Stupid tears leaked onto her cheeks. Lindy swiped furiously at them with the too-long sleeve of her sweater. "Jarrett," she yelled. "Jarrett, come back! You still owe me eighteen lousy hours."

But he was already gone, the front door slamming behind him. For the second time that day, he'd left her.

THE PICKETERS MARCHED back and forth in front of Nick's trailer, waving their signs: DOWN WITH ALDRIDGE AVIATION! RESCUE THE OWLS! PROTECT THE HELPLESS! FEATHER POWER!

Lindy had hardly slept three nights in a row, working around the clock to organize this protest—so far her one answer to Juliet's nefarious proposal. Several of her students who hadn't gone home for summer break had pitched in to help her. Chief among them was Eric Sotelo. He'd done the signs with great care, using tempera paints and the very best bristol board. These were truly the most well-crafted signs a person could hope to see at a protest rally. Eric hid behind one of them now, peering out at Lindy with a wistful expression. She smiled at him and he popped back behind SAVE OUR BURROWS! Did he really have a crush on her? Blast Nick Jarrett for even mentioning the possibility. The man had disrupted every aspect of her life.

She hadn't seen Nick since that miserable night when Juliet had come to her house. But she yearned to see him. She kept remembering how his golden brown hair ignited in the sunlight, and how his eyes could turn dark with desire. She remembered the way he talked about airplanes, as if there could be nothing

more grand in the world than to take flight in a plane
of his own design. Basically, Lindy missed Nick. She
felt deprived, like someone impoverished who
dreamed of unattainable riches. What might have
happened between them—it was useless to speculate
about that anymore! But Lindy went on speculating
and imagining. And it hurt.

"Professor Mac! We're already running out of
doughnuts. What'll we do?" The voice of one of Lindy's students interrupted this latest reverie about Nick.
Goodness, she had to get to work. Keeping a protest
rally in top form was no easy task. For the next hour
or so she rushed around, solving one crisis after another. She'd advertised free refreshments for anyone
willing to carry a placard, and more volunteers were
arriving all the time. She dispatched Eric into town to
buy some chocolate-chip cookies and blueberry Danish. Then the entire Santiago Future Leaders Club
showed up—several ten-year-old boys and girls who
were happy to holler at the top of their lungs whenever they marched past a window. Everything was fine
until the Future Leaders tried climbing en masse onto
the roof of the trailer. Just as that particular situation
was resolved, Hammersmith came careering up to
Lindy after chasing jackrabbits. He knocked over one
of the refreshment tables, sending tropical punch everywhere. Eric went back into town, this time for
cherry soda and root beer.

Lindy stood beside Nick's truck, wiping tropical
punch from the front of her shirt. Parked next to the
truck was a gaudy van painted all over with scenes of
girls in bikinis. The van had been sitting here ever since
Lindy had arrived this morning. She knew it well. It

was one of the more distinctive vehicles from the Ee-zee Go Auto rental agency in downtown Santiago. Stories were already circulating about some wild red-headed woman who'd rented the van and was seen cruising Main Street at odd hours of the night.

Lindy turned and stared at Nick's trailer. All the curtains were drawn tight. So far there had been no sign of reaction to the picketers, not even a twitch of a curtain. Nick used the trailer for his office, but it was also his temporary home. To think of him in there with Juliet, all snug and comfortable... Lindy wanted to sprint right up to the trailer door and bang on it with all her might. But that wouldn't be a dignified sort of protest. Not appropriate or professional in the least.

Lindy marched around the trailer. Periodically she raised her megaphone and bellowed into it. "We need more picketers on the south side—there's a gap in the line!... Would the Future Leaders please stop throw-ing spitballs?... Don't forget the raffle at twelve noon sharp. Grand prize is a Down with Aldridge Aviation T-shirt!"

Hammersmith bounded off to chase more rabbits. The Future Leaders disappeared, only to be discov-ered later trying to dismantle Juliet's van. With them were three empty cookie boxes; Eric made yet an-other trip into town. The picketers started singing work songs, beads of perspiration trickling down their faces in the hot sun. They sounded horrible. And at last a head popped out of the door of the trailer, frizzy red hair seeming to quiver in outrage.

"MacAllister!"

Lindy raised her megaphone. "Yes?"

"Put that stupid thing away and get in here. It's time to talk."

Lindy set her megaphone down, climbed the steps of the trailer and went inside. The air here was almost cold, blowing at her from the swamp cooler. She took off her baseball cap and pushed the hair away from her face, walking toward the kitchen. Juliet slapped along right behind her, but all Lindy could do was gaze at Nick.

He sat at the kitchen table, surrounded by his blue-prints and file folders and coffee mugs. His haircut was starting to settle down; it didn't appear quite so raw anymore. And he hadn't shaved yet. He was growing a luxuriant golden beard. Not only that, he was wearing his ankle-high chukka boots and his camouflage shirt with the sleeves rolled up. Perhaps his trousers were the expensively tailored kind, but they only added to his rugged attractiveness.

Lindy was hot, sticky and thirsty right now, but looking at Nick was enough to make her feel wonderfully refreshed. She nearly smiled at him. Unfortunately, he didn't act at all happy to see *her*. He barely even glanced at her.

"Do you think you're going to accomplish anything with this latest stunt of yours?" He scowled into his coffee cup.

"Yes, I do. The tide of public opinion is turning against Aldridge Aviation. We're prepared to picket until you change the factory location!"

Juliet stood over at the counter, rattling the coffee-pot in a disturbing manner. Yet, surprisingly, she made no comment of her own. Meanwhile, the sound of off-key singing blared into the trailer. Nick groaned and rubbed both hands through his hair.

"How the heck are we supposed to get any work done with all this racket going on?"

"That's the point, I believe," Lindy remarked in a caustic tone.

Finally he gave her his full attention, his disapproving gaze sweeping over her. She was suddenly conscious of the tropical-punch stains and the sweat-dampened tumble of hair around her face. But she refused to look away from him. They stared at each other.

"Confound it, Professor, why can't you be rational for once? I've tried to resolve this whole thing sensibly—"

"You haven't tried beans! Oh, you thought you could placate me with your twenty-four-hour plan. But you never intended to take *that* seriously. By the way, you still owe me at least eighteen hours. Shows just how much effort you've put in so far."

Lindy moved closer to the table. Nick pushed his chair back, standing up and taking a stride toward her. They stood toe-to-toe, glaring at each other in the middle of the kitchen. Juliet was doing mysterious things with the coffeepot, but she glanced at Nick and Lindy with a nasty little smirk. Obviously she was enjoying their argument. Lindy didn't want to give the woman any more entertainment. Nick, however, seemed oblivious to anything but his own disgust with Lindy.

"Let's get a few things straight," he said. "That cockeyed plan about spending twenty-four hours together was your idea in the first place. I did my best to comply. I came over to your house that night, didn't I? Completely prepared to fulfill my end of the bargain.''

"Ha. All you did was make accusations. And then you just left. You know what really burns me up, Jarrett? I'll tell you what. You think you have me all figured out. You think I'm rigid and uncompromising. You think I can't ever change. Well, maybe I have changed this past couple of weeks. Only you haven't bothered to find out about it!'' Now Lindy didn't give a hoot if Juliet was listening. The coffeepot began to produce a strange sort of boiling, and Lindy herself was starting to boil with indignation. She poked an accusing finger right at Nick's chest. "It so happens *you're* the one who's rigid and uncompromising. You haven't given an inch. And I've given far too much already.''

"Okay, Professor. Exactly what is it you've given? How did you change? You're right, I don't see it. So tell me about it.'' Nick's voice was harsh. Lindy realized her finger was still poking at him, as if it would do anything to linger near his camouflaged chest.

Nick was waiting for an answer, but she found she couldn't offer him one, after all. How could she possibly tell him that she'd changed by falling in love with him? She couldn't risk saying those words out loud. She wouldn't be able to bear it if Nick rejected her, so she said nothing at all. She and Nick merely went on glaring at each other, close enough for an embrace or a kiss. And then Nick stepped even closer to her, as if he *would* kiss her in spite of his anger—

"Romeo, dear, here's your coffee.'' Juliet nudged her way between the two of them, pushing yet another coffee mug under Nick's nose. He grimaced, but took the mug.

"Do you have to keep calling me that?"

"You know I do." Juliet rested her hand intimately on his shoulder. It was a large square hand with freckles. Lindy wanted to swat it away from Nick as if it were a big ugly bug. She had a difficult time restraining herself. Darn it, why didn't he move away from Juliet, instead of standing there next to her so companionably?

But as he gulped her coffee, his entire face puckered up. He looked like he'd swallowed mud. It took a moment for his features to rearrange themselves into a normal expression. "Uh, Juliet...I thought my own coffee was bad enough. But yours... Besides, I don't see why you're getting domestic all of a sudden, anyway."

"I'm full of surprises." Juliet squeezed his shoulder while favoring Lindy with a toothy grin. Lindy swung her purse back and forth, steadying herself with its weight. Juliet Aldridge certainly didn't seem the type of woman who would be happy making coffee for a man and serving it to him, as well. What was she up to?

Now Juliet trotted over to the kitchen window and stared outside. "Oh, dear, I thought I heard something strange. Romeo, some of those odious children are trying to pry the window right out of its frame. Go away, you hooligans!"

Muffled shrieks could be heard from outside. Nick frowned.

"What the devil—"

"You'd better get out there and stop them," Juliet urged. "Hurry, before they take apart the entire place."

Nick gave Lindy an acid look. "Can't you keep discipline in your own ranks, Professor?"

"Um . . . they're supposed to cause as much trouble as possible. Those are their instructions." Lindy peered uneasily around Juliet, trying to see exactly how much damage the Future Leaders were inflicting. But Juliet blocked the window, another big grin on her face.

"All right," Nick muttered. "This mayhem has gone far enough. I'm going to put a stop to it." He strode out of the trailer. Lindy started to follow him, but Juliet intervened with speed and dexterity. Just as Nick went out the door, she closed it after him and shot the bolt into place.

"There. Now you and I can have a confidential chat, Linden. Girl talk, you know. Things we wouldn't want anyone else to hear."

"So that was just a ploy to get Nick out of here," Lindy said contemptuously.

"Oh, he'll have his hands full. Your little angels *are* causing a ruckus. But that's all to our advantage. It'll give us the time we need for our talk. Come along." And Juliet sailed down the hallway to a room at the end of the trailer.

Lindy stayed by the door a moment, ready to march outside. And yet she'd have to deal with Juliet sooner or later. It would probably be best to get this unpleasant task out of the way right now.

With an explosive sigh, Lindy went to the room at the end of the hall. It had only one piece of furniture—a rumpled bed that took up most of the available space. Juliet plunked herself down on it.

"I believe you have some explaining to do, Linden. When I offered you a compromise solution to your owl problem, I never said anything about allowing this little protest march."

"Somehow it slipped my mind to ask your permission. Too bad." Lindy glanced around. She didn't like being here—in Nick's bedroom. Like the rest of the trailer, it was a sterile, anonymous place, even more uninspiring than a hotel room. But it was also the one place that hinted at Nick's own personality. He'd tacked some oversize photographs to the walls, all of them showing airplanes in flight. And on one wall hung a poster of an ancient boxy-winged plane, people in Edwardian dress posing beside it. The poster was creased and faded, as if Nick had owned it for a very long time and carried it around with him wherever he went. Lindy was glimpsing a special corner of his life, yet without his consent.

"There must be somewhere else we can talk," she declared. "Another room."

"It's a small trailer. And I'm running out of patience. Do you have an answer for me, or what? Your owls or Nick. Choose!"

Lindy folded her arms and leaned back against the wall. She regarded Juliet coolly. "No. I won't choose. You can't manipulate me, no matter how hard you try. Besides, you just don't have that much power over Nick. Sooner or later he'll realize he's felt guilty enough about the Happy Blossom Wedding Chapel."

For a second a new emotion flickered across Juliet's face. Could it be uncertainty? But this glimpse of vulnerability was gone as quickly as it had come.

"You don't get it, Linden. You think all Nick feels for me is a sense of obligation. You don't realize what good friends we've been all these years. Together, the two of us, building up Aldridge Aviation. The struggles, the hard times we've been through—and the good times, the successes. We've shared all of it. That's not something that goes away."

Lindy stiffened. "I don't care if you and Nick went to kindergarten together. I won't negotiate with you."

Juliet widened her eyes. "Well, now. You're giving up on the owls, just like that? Maybe you don't care about them much, after all."

Lindy straightened up. "I'm still going to save them. Listen to those people out there! They'll stand behind me. You can't fight all of us."

Juliet gave her throaty laugh. "Kiddo, you're even more naive than I thought. Your friends will stick around until they get tired and bored. Then they'll go home and forget all about you. And that brings it back to just the three of us. Me, you and Nick. Since I'm a generous person, I'll give you one more chance to decide. What'll it be—Nick or the owls?"

Lindy was dismayed to find herself wavering. She knew the odds were against her. She wasn't naive, contrary to Juliet's opinion. She realized a lot of her supporters were here because of the free cookies, and because a protest rally was something novel. Lindy also knew that most people in Santiago still wanted the jobs Aldridge Aviation would provide. Her battle was a lonely one, perhaps even an impossible one. If she

gave up Nick, the owls would be safe—and she'd be
safe, too. She'd hurt for a very long time, but she'd
have the best excuse in the world for retreating from
love....

BAM! BAM! BAM! The knocking on the front
door made Lindy jump.

"Let me in," Nick bellowed. "What the heck is going on in there?"

And right then, listening to him, Lindy knew she
could not go through her life without listening to him
some more. She'd come to know his voice in all its in-
flections. She'd heard it brimming with humor, low
and husky with desire...and downright cranky, the
way it was now. She had to go on hearing Nick's voice.
It was as simple and elemental as that. She turned back
to Juliet with new resolve.

"I can't believe I'd even consider your pathetic
compromise. This choice you're giving me—it's
wrong, that's what it is. I couldn't live with myself if
I made any kind of bargain with you. So here's *my*
choice. I'm going to fight you for the owls, and I'm
going to fight you for Nick!" Exhilaration swept
through Lindy, and she shook her purseful of rocks to
give emphasis to her pronouncement. She felt strong,
and all she had to do was believe in her own strength
and fight Juliet Aldridge.

Juliet plopped back against Nick's pillows. She
laughed again. "Mercy me. This is a development I
clearly didn't anticipate. But I like it, anyway. It's
good when people take me by surprise. This is as much
fun as a hockey game, Linden. You're keeping my
skate blades sharp." She lapsed into a silence of obvious contentment. Nick could be heard rattling the

front door and grumbling vociferously. That didn't seem to bother Juliet at all. She merely kicked off her shoes and stretched her muscular legs. Today she was wearing another jumpsuit, this one bright purple with white pinstripes and a double row of buttons down the front. It looked like it had started out trying to be a tuxedo, then lost its initiative and decided to be a pair of pajamas instead. Lindy stared at Juliet's multicolored toenails, not trusting the woman's relaxed mood. She sensed trickery in Juliet, as keenly as a wild creature might catch the scent of unseen danger in the air.

Juliet rolled onto her side, propping her head against one hand. "This is a comfortable bed. Extremely comfortable. Of course, I already knew that from recent experience."

Lindy bent the brim of her baseball cap. "What are you implying? Whatever devious thing you have in mind, spit it out straight."

"Why do you think I brought you into the bedroom? We both know exactly what I'm implying. How can I spell it out any better? It's like I told you. Nicholas and I, we're the best of friends. We're also lovers. We have been for a long time, and we still are."

Lindy's stomach churned in revulsion. "I don't believe you. This is another one of your schemes, that's all."

Juliet ran her hand slowly over the mattress. "You don't know for sure, though, do you? Maybe I *am* telling the truth. And when you think about it, why wouldn't I be? I keep trying to get something across to you, Linden. I'm not a devious person. I'm very straightforward. Sure, I'll fight dirty when I have to.

But it'll be out in the open. You'll always be able to see me coming at you."

It was easy to picture Juliet in a hockey uniform, hunched low as she sliced across the ice with her stick, slamming into other players with glee. But she was devious; Lindy had no doubt about that. Juliet lolled on Nick's bed, her bright red hair fanning across one of the pillows. Her smile was secretive, mischievous, as if she was delighted with the terrible seed of doubt she'd planted in Lindy's mind.

Yes, the doubt was there; could it possibly be that Juliet was telling the truth, after all? That she and Nick...

"I don't believe you," Lindy repeated, but even to her own ears the words sounded hollow and frail. Her brief moment of triumph had vanished, replaced by turmoil and bitterness. Juliet had seen to that.

Lindy couldn't stay in this room any longer. Not with Juliet draped across Nick's bed like a big, exotic purple flower. Lindy hurried down the hall, Juliet's hearty laugh echoing after her. She yanked open the front door.

"What in tarnation is going on?" Nick complained, barreling past her into the trailer. "I finally get those kids into line, and then I'm locked out of my own house. Great. What do you have planned for me next?"

She gazed at him, desperately needing reassurance that he wasn't Juliet's lover. But once again she couldn't say out loud what was innermost in her heart. She was too afraid. How did she know whether or not she could trust Nick? How did she really know?

When at last she spoke, her throat was dry and aching. "Ask Juliet your questions, Nick. I can't tell you anything."

"Lindy—"

"I can't talk to you. I have a protest rally waiting for me. Nothing else is important right now!" And with that she fled out of the trailer, away from the man she loved.

CHAPTER ELEVEN

"LINDY, FOR THE HUNDREDTH time—will you come in?" Nick stood on the stoop of his trailer, the last fading light of day sparking flame in his tousled hair. Lindy looked away from him and went on tramping back and forth with her FEATHER POWER! placard propped against her shoulder. Her feet ached. She was tired and discouraged, but she would not give up this battle. Never! The owls were depending on her.

"It's getting late and everyone else has gone home," Nick pointed out. "Don't you think you're carrying things a little far?"

It was true that her supporters had left, one by one, just as Juliet had predicted. Even the Future Leaders had been bused back into town by a frazzled parent. In the end only Eric Sotelo had remained, still hiding behind his sign, but stalwart as he wore a path around and around the trailer. It had taken a great deal of effort for Lindy to convince him he needed to go home to eat supper. Much as she'd appreciated all his help, it was a relief not to have him peering at her with that dreamy, admiring expression.

"Your mutt's in here with me. You might as well come in, too. What will it hurt you to rest a while? Then you can go back to your damn fool picketing."

Hammersmith could be seen in the doorway behind Nick, wagging his floppy tail. He'd catapulted into the trailer some time ago—when Juliet had stormed outside and neglected to close the door. Juliet had looked furious, her face a vivid red that rivaled the color of her hair. After giving Lindy one scathing glance, she'd climbed into her van and roared away, the paintings of girls in bikinis obscured by a cloud of dust. Lindy could only imagine what had transpired between Juliet and Nick.

"I'll fix you dinner," he said now. "Hamburgers and pickles. How can you resist?"

Her mouth watered. She hadn't had anything to eat the entire day except for doughnuts, chocolate-chip cookies and half a blueberry Danish. After all that sugar she was like a creature in need of a salt lick. Propping her sign on the ground, she leaned against it.

"I didn't know you could cook, Jarrett."

"I can't. But that never stopped me before." He stuffed his hands into the pockets of his trousers, standing there astride the stoop like a man in front of a castle, not a trailer. The love inside Lindy swelled; no crescendo of music could have been more poignant. Her love was painful, a torment. So much stood between her and Nick. How could she ever surmount the obstacles? The battle over the factory site, the suspicions Juliet had cast today, Lindy's terrible feeling that Nick couldn't ever love her in return, her fear of betrayal...

No way would it be a good idea to go inside that trailer tonight. She'd only be asking for more pain. But Nick was silhouetted in the doorway, tall and strong, beckoning to her heart. She allowed her protest sign to fall to the ground. Wearily she climbed the steps of the trailer, stumbling a little. Nick took hold of her, and Hammersmith threw his furry yellow body against her as if he hadn't seen her in a week. For a moment Lindy was caught between the two of them, Nick and Hammers—warmed by this contact that was both human and canine. An exuberant tongue rasped across her cheek, a firm hand steered her by the elbow. With so much help she ended up in an awkward heap on the sofa. Hammersmith climbed into her lap, obviously suffering the delusion he was no bigger than a toy poodle. His weight knocked Lindy's breath away, but she held on to him for emotional support. Nick surveyed her.

"You look rotten, Professor."

"Thanks." She made an unsuccessful attempt to smooth her windblown hair.

"I know what it is. You're probably dehydrated after marching around like a half-wit in the sun all day."

"Thanks again."

He brought her a glass of ice water from the kitchen. She took a long drink.

"Thanks. And this time I really mean it."

Hammers snuffled her glass as she drank some more. Nick gave the dog a disapproving glance, but filled a large bowl of water at the sink and plunked it down on the kitchen floor. Hammers leapt joyfully from Lindy's lap, knocking her arm and spilling the glass of water all over her. She gasped at the cold shock, reminded of the way it felt to jump into an unheated swimming pool. But maybe this would help wash out the tropical-punch stains on her clothes.

Without saying a word, Nick tossed her a wrinkled dish towel. She did her best to dry herself off. Meanwhile, Hammers finished taking his own drink and splashed a paw into his water bowl. The bowl went tipping over on its side, and the kitchen floor instantly turned into a small lake.

"Oh, no!" Lindy scrambled over and began mopping the floor with her dish towel. Hammers frolicked beside her, helping to spread the water into as yet untouched corners. Nick watched both of them in ominous silence, like a bomb that couldn't decide whether to explode or to fizzle out in defeat. After a moment he waded out of the kitchen; when he returned, he tossed some bath towels onto the floor and started his own mopping operation.

He and Lindy worked side by side on their hands and knees, Hammersmith licking each of their faces by turn.

"Is life always this exciting with your mutt around?"

"Usually. But tell me this. Is life always exciting when Juliet's around?" Lindy slid her sodden towel over the floor with renewed vigor. She had to know what Juliet meant to Nick. No matter how hurtful the truth might be, anything was better than the agony she'd put herself through all day—wondering, hoping, despairing.

Nick glanced at her sharply as he wrung out a corner of a towel. "I couldn't get any answers from Juliet today. She won't say a word about what's going on between you two. Are *you* going to explain any of it?"

"No." Lindy gazed at the water still eddying around her. It had turned muddy from the dirt on Hammersmith's paws. She leaned back on the heels of her hiking boots. "If you and Juliet are so close, why can't you get her to talk to you? The way I understand it, you're the best of friends. And more!" The words tumbled out of her, angry and accusing.

"What the heck are you talking about?" Nick demanded. "These days Juliet and I can't even say hello without an argument."

"Maybe the two of you get along better in bed." Lindy's voice trembled. She hated the things she was saying, hated the need that made her say them. Nick straightened up and frowned at her.

"Is that what you think? That Juliet and I..."

"It's what she said. Why shouldn't I believe her? And why should I care, blast it?" Lindy slapped the floor with her wet towel, spraying both herself and Nick. He took hold of her wrist.

"Lindy, I'm not sleeping with Juliet."

"How do I know that?" she asked miserably. "How do I know anything!"

"Maybe you have to take a chance." His voice was rough. "Maybe you have to trust me. Maybe, once and for all, you have to tell yourself I'm not the Cluny."

"I've tried," she whispered. "I want to believe you...."

"Then believe."

"You make it sound so simple!"

"It is, Lindy."

She shook her head. "Not with you and me, Nick. It's not simple at all. We don't believe in fighting for the same things. We'll never get close enough to have the kind of trust you're talking about. Where does that leave us?"

He released her abruptly. "Don't ask me. I only know that I want you, Lindy. More than I've ever wanted any woman. Does that make sense? No. It sure as hell doesn't." He shoved his own towel across the floor. Hammersmith attacked the towel, apparently thinking this was some new game. He dug into it with his teeth, growling as he shook it enthusiastically. More muddy water sprayed over Nick and Lindy. But neither one of them spoke now. Tension pulsed between them like the vibration sent underground by a roaring train.

Lindy glanced over at Nick as he took another towel and mopped up more water with a vengeance. She couldn't look away from him, captivated by the gold hair of his forearms, the corded muscles working underneath. His features were taut as he stared back at her. And Lindy knew that if she made one move toward him, one gesture of capitulation, she'd be crushed in his arms, right where she longed to be. Yet she held back, struggling to stay safe. Nick desired her...but did he love her? Even if he *could* love her some day, how would that resolve all the conflicts between them? Oh, why did everything have to be so darn complicated!

Somehow Lindy wrenched her gaze from Nick. The moment of intimacy that had flashed between them was gone, taken by her fears. She flapped her towel at Hammersmith to distract him from licking her face. And hurriedly she went on mopping, careful not to look at Nick anymore.

At last the kitchen was only somewhat damp, all the soggy towels lumped together in a bucket. Hammers trotted into the living room, probably hoping to cause new commotion. Lindy struggled to her feet, watching as Nick stood, also. The knees of his expensive pants were wet and dirty.

She reached down to pick up the bowl Hammers had knocked over. "Thanks for the water. It really, uh, quenched our thirst. But Hammers and I have to get back to our protest."

"Stay right where you are," Nick commanded. "I still owe you those eighteen hours, and I never go back on a deal. You hear?" He glanced around belligerently, as if ready to stave off arguments from Lindy, Hammersmith or anyone else who dared to challenge him. "So, how do you like your hamburgers? Medium, rare, or well done?"

Some time later Nick and Lindy sat across from each other at the kitchen table. Two burnt and shriveled hamburgers huddled on Lindy's plate like lumps of coal. In spite of the culinary choices offered by Nick, it appeared that "well done" was the only option. But the hamburgers tasted delicious once they were smothered in catsup and mustard.

Hammersmith had already eaten three burgers straight. He'd been banished outside after propping his chin on the table and gazing hopefully at Nick's plate. Now he could be heard moaning at the window, but Lindy was so exhausted she found it easy to ignore him. She slumped back in her chair, munching on a pickle. She frowned at Nick's work papers that had been pushed to one side of the table, wishing she could tear up all these documents about the Aldridge

Aviation factory site. But then her eye was caught by a whimsical sketch sticking out between two file folders, and she pulled it toward her. It depicted a small, snub-nosed plane with stubby wings and a rounded tail. An old-fashioned sort of airplane, drawn in a few quick lines that somehow managed to express the joy of flying. For Lindy could tell the little plane was soaring in the air, not remaining demurely earthbound.

"You drew this, didn't you?" she asked.

"I was doodling. I didn't exactly get a lot of productive work done today." He tried to take the sketch from her, but she held on to it. She couldn't stop looking at it, as if it could tell her something she needed to know. What it finally *did* tell her wasn't welcome at all.

"You and Juliet," she murmured, still staring at the sketch. "No matter what else happens, the two of you share a love of flying. That kind of bond, it's not so easily broken, is it?"

Nick rubbed his beard. "Sure, that's why Juliet and I started out being such good friends, because of the way we both feel about airplanes. But what does that have to do with anything right now?"

"When I was with you on the mesa, *we* were sharing something. We really were. Then Juliet came in her helicopter. And what you share with her became more important to you." Lindy set down her pickle, no longer hungry. She pushed back her chair and stood. For a moment she was tempted to crumple up Nick's sketch of the airplane and toss it down. Instead, contrarily, she folded it in half and stuffed it into her shirt pocket. Then she glanced at her watch and strode across the kitchen linoleum, her boots making squishy noises in the spots where dampness lingered. She went to the living room and switched on the television set.

"I'm going to be on the news," she said stiffly. "I don't want to miss it."

Nick came to stand behind her, distracting her. She wished he would go away somewhere and leave her alone. But this was his house, after all. Lindy folded her arms, pressing them against her body. She'd called several reporters in Albuquerque to announce her protest march, and one of them had traveled out this afternoon to interview her. Now she waited impatiently for her story to come on the air. First she had to listen to the national headlines, then all the local stories. Those perky anchor people just rambled on and on.

Lindy took a step toward the television set, as if that would hurry up things. What was taking so long? By now the show had petered down to the section where humorous oddities and lighthearted events were reported—like the chili-pepper contest in Valencia County. On the screen a little girl was shown proudly holding up the giant green pepper that had won her first prize. Darn it all, Lindy's owls belonged with the serious news stories!

At last the television camera panned across Nick's trailer, zooming in on the reporter who'd interviewed Lindy.

"A war is being waged in Santiago, New Mexico," intoned the reporter. "The battleground is one small section of mesa where burrowing owls must fight for their existence against the encroachment of a new factory. Professor Linden MacAllister of the Chamberlin Institute of Technology has taken up the cause of the burrowers."

The camera switched to Lindy, who spoke seriously and intensely to all the television viewers: "Please, we need everyone's support. Do a few little burrowing owls matter? Yes, they do! Don't let their homes be destroyed." She went on talking about the owls, once again using every technique she'd learned in lecture halls to stir jaded students.

Lindy gazed at her own image. Her forceful presence on the screen was undermined by a fuzzy yellow head floating up and down in the background. Boing...boing...boing! Hammersmith's face punctuated her speech at odd moments, reminding her of those old cartoons where a little ball would bounce along on top of some song lyrics. Well, Hammers certainly added some liveliness to the scene. Then Lindy's image was gone, replaced by that of the reporter.

"The battle of Santiago will continue," he proclaimed. "Who will win—the powerful Goliath in the form of Aldridge Aviation? Or an improbable David—Professor Linden MacAllister, champion of owls?" Behind the reporter Hammersmith's head popped into view, one ear cocked straight up as if receiving transmissions from outer space. Poor Hammers could get the silliest grin on his snout. But now the weather lady had taken over, predicting more sunny days. Lindy switched off the television set and turned to face Nick.

"You see? We're really starting to get some attention. A lot of people told me they'd be back to picket tomorrow, and I'm sure we'll have fresh recruits, as

well. You and Juliet don't stand a chance." She spoke
with more confidence than she felt. Certainly she
didn't tell Nick about the indignant town councillors
who'd cornered her outside the trailer today—chief
among them Melanie Deams. There was still a lot of
public support for Aldridge Aviation. But somehow
Lindy had to keep up her spirits. She needed strength
to go on fighting!

"So you were good on the news," Nick muttered.
"You have a perverse talent for eloquence, no deny-
ing that. Okay. Fine. But I already told you, I never go
back on a deal. I agreed to get this factory built at
minimum cost and maximum efficiency. And that's
what I'm going to do." In spite of these emphatic
words, Nick looked perturbed and out of sorts. He
prowled around his small living room as if too restless
to stand still. Then he came back to Lindy.

"I need to go flying," he said urgently. "It's been
too long since I was in the air. Come with me, Professor."

"What—right now? At night?"

"Night flying is the best. I've got my plane out at
the Santiago airfield, ready and waiting. Well, what do
you say?" His face had come alive; it was amazing
how even the thought of taking off in an airplane
seemed to bring him so much happiness. But Lindy
hated to fly. Put her on a mountain and she'd scale a
rock slope with eagerness. Put her in an airplane and
she'd start looking for the nearest parachute.

"I can't go with you," she told Nick firmly. "First
of all, I have Hammersmith with me, and—"

"We'll drop him off at your house. It's right on the
way to the airfield. Couldn't work out better."

"Maybe some other time."

Nick didn't seem to hear her. He grasped her by the shoulders, his eyes shining with a color like sun-washed sky. "You've been right about one thing all along. More than anything, I want to fly. Just that simple and basic. I want to fly. Somehow I've gotten caught up in all this other stuff. But not tonight. To-night it'll be as simple as it was meant to be. Come with me, Lindy."

She tried to think of an excuse that would sound reasonable to him. But again she seemed to hear Ju-liet's mischievous laughter echoing in the trailer, a sound of triumph. And that decided it. If Lindy could share this one thing with Nick—his love of flying—she could offer him as much as Juliet did. Perhaps more. That thought alone was enough to sway Lindy in fa-vor of airplanes.

"Yes," she told Nick. "Yes, I'll go flying with you!"

LINDY DUG INTO HER PURSE, grabbing an entire handful of rocks. She forced herself to breathe deeply and slowly. There, that was better. But she still felt as if she was hanging suspended in some dark and terri-ble void. Even though the plane's engines thrummed steadily, she experienced no sense of motion through the night. It was awful, not being able to see anything out there beyond the windows. Only a blackness that surely would suck the plane down into nothingness.

"Does this airplane have a name?" Lindy asked, making an effort to calm her nerves.

Nick was evasive. "You think just because you call your car Sally, other people are wacky, too?"

"Out with it, Jarrett. What's the name of this airplane?"

He cleared his throat and mumbled something that sounded like "Falumph."

"What did you say?"

"Finola. That's it, all right? Are you satisfied? She came with that name when I bought her. There wasn't anything I could do about it."

Finola, Finola. It sounded like some bizarre type of breakfast cereal. Lindy's stomach felt queasy. She stared at the instrument panel, trying to make sense out of it. But that was a mistake. She started to think she saw the needles of all those gauges quivering in alarm. She took another deep breath.

"We've been up here quite a while, haven't we?" she asked with forced nonchalance.

"Not nearly long enough. I could fly for hours. Takes the strain right out of me." He gave a sigh of contentment, settling back in his seat. "There's nothing like winging a night sky. I remember how excited I was when I got my instrument rating. That was almost better than my first solo flight. Say, do you want to take the wheel?"

"You've got to be kidding."

"Not at all. That's the only way you'll find out how much fun flying is. Go ahead—put your hands on the wheel. That's all. Get the feel of it."

Lindy regarded the wheel in front of her, identical to Nick's. It wasn't actually a wheel; rather, it was two arms curving upward like a muscleman showing off his biceps. Maybe it wouldn't be so bad to maneuver the thing a little. What she disliked most about flying was being out of control. Very well, then. Tonight she'd take some control. She grasped both arms of the wheel. Before she knew it, she'd jerked it to the left. Now she did feel the plane move—way too much! Her stomach seemed to vault in the opposite direction, as if in protest.

"Whoa," said Nick, taking over again. "This baby's not like a car. All she needs is a very light touch. But didn't that feel great?"

It *had* felt exhilarating, for the merest second. And maybe it would have been fun to try some more. But unfortunately Lindy's stomach wasn't cooperating. She glanced over at Nick. He seemed perfectly at home, perfectly happy. She hated to ruin things for him, but she didn't have any choice. Blast! She'd so wanted this flight to work out.

The plane pitched, and Lindy's stomach pitched, too.

"Nick, we have a problem,"

"That was just some turbulence. The air is a little rough over the mesa."

"No, no, it's not the turbulence, it's my stomach. I think I'm going to be sick."

"It was my hamburgers," he said instantly. "This isn't the first time my cooking hasn't gone down right. Lord, I'm sorry."

Her teeth were starting to chatter. "Actually, I think I'm airsick."

"No, it's my hamburgers. Trust me."

She held a hand to her stomach. "Whatever it is, I feel crummy. You might as well know...I get nervous when I fly. And I'm talking really nervous. Especially at night, when I can't see anything." She was losing her cool, the last thing she wanted to do in an airplane with Nick. But he reached across the cockpit toward her, taking her hand in his.

"Don't worry," he murmured. "Trust me, Professor. I'll keep you safe."

That's what he'd been asking all along—he'd been asking for her trust. And she hadn't been able to give it to him. Not until this moment, anyway. Because, miraculously, at his touch she began to relax a little. Even her stomach started to settle down. Somehow she knew that Nick would keep her safe, just as he'd promised. She gripped his hand.

"I do trust you. I believe what you told me tonight, about you and Juliet. I know you're not like the Cluny. I can finally say that with all my heart."

She'd admitted enough. She had to stop, before she revealed too much. But already she was blurting out the rest of it. "Nick, I know we don't have a whole lot in common. Maybe not anything! You want to build that factory, I'm determined to stop you. You like planes, I hate the darn things. Give me a good rock any day. Even so, I can't help myself. I love you. That's all there is to it. I love you."

She knew the words were a mistake as soon as she'd uttered them. Nick didn't answer, his fingers tensing under hers. Oh, damn! On solid ground she would have been able to control herself. But being trapped up here in this Finola airplane left her feeling vulnerable, with only Nick to cling to. Most humiliating of all, she went on clinging to him. She couldn't let go of his hand.

"Lindy, I don't know what to tell you," he said at last, his voice low. "You've got me twisted into loops. I don't know how I feel about you. I go crazy when

I'm with you...I go crazy when I'm *not* with you. What kind of sense am I supposed to make out of that?''

"Don't say any more," she whispered. "If you can't tell me you love me...don't say any more."

He didn't speak. He held her hand a few more moments in his warm, reassuring grasp, and then he turned the plane back toward the lights of Santiago. Lindy was very calm, with nothing but a cold heaviness inside her. Flying seemed an insignificant thing compared to the devastating truth that faced her now.

Nick Jarrett did not love her.

CHAPTER TWELVE

THE BULLDOZER LUMBERED over the mesa like some prehistoric monster, its shovel a hungry, gaping mouth. Lindy punched down on the gas pedal of her little blue car and raced in front of the bulldozer, blocking its path. She gripped Sally's steering wheel, hunching low to peer out the windshield. From here she could see that the driver of the machine was a heavyset man with a dour face. He looked uncomfortable and obviously wasn't pleased to be caught in the Battle of Santiago—as Lindy's feud with Aldridge Aviation was now commonly known. But Lindy couldn't help the man's ill ease. All her efforts to stop Aldridge had come down to this one morning, when construction was scheduled to begin on the factory. She couldn't let it happen!

The bulldozer backed up awkwardly and rumbled in a new direction. Lindy cranked her steering wheel and charged to block the monstrous machine. She was breathing hard, as if she'd just sprinted across the mesa. Her hands were slippery on the wheel, and she wiped them on her jeans. She wondered despairingly if she shouldn't have accepted Juliet's proposal, after all. Relinquish Nick, save the owls...

Lindy set her mouth in a grim line. Not even for the sake of the poor owls could she compromise her in-

tegrity by bargaining with Juliet. And she couldn't relinquish someone who didn't belong to her. It had
been a whole week since her confession of love to
Nick, a whole week of his silence. Oh, she'd continued to picket his trailer with her supporters, and she'd
argued with him countless times about the owls. After all, he'd been determined to live up to his twenty-
four-hour agreement with her. But he'd never said
anything about loving her—not a hint, not a hope.
And now the final stage of their battle was set. Somehow Lindy had to keep the owls safe.

The bulldozer backed up yet again, starting a new
tack. Lindy's car darted, nimble as a spider, barring
the way. The heavyset man threw up both hands. He
clambered down from the bulldozer and hurried toward the group of townspeople beginning to gather on
the edge of the factory site. Lindy saw him reach Nick;
the two men stood together in deep conversation for
a moment. Lindy focused on a bright, frizzy thatch of
red hair rising above the crowd. No doubt Juliet was
enjoying herself, probably laughing at Lindy's efforts
to stall construction. Well, she could laugh all she
liked. Because Lindy wasn't going to budge. Not ever.

Nick had turned and was striding toward Lindy, a
stony expression on his face that chilled her. In case he
tried to remove her physically from the car, she locked
the door and cranked up her window. As he drew
nearer, she was dismayed to see that he'd shaved off
his beard. His jaw looked unguarded, exposed—yet
very stubborn.

He surprised her. Instead of coming to argue, he
swung up into the seat of the bulldozer, acting as if he
knew how to drive the wretched beast. And then he

was driving it—straight toward Lindy. He lowered the scoop and gouged it into the earth, piling dirt against her car. Sally tilted up a fraction... then a fraction more. What did Nick Jarrett think he was doing?

"Stop!" she yelled in fury, cranking her window down. But already Nick had ruthlessly immobilized her car with this pile of dirt. Backing up with a roar of the bulldozer's engine, he headed straight toward Lindy's foxhole—and the owls' burrows.

"No! You can't do it, Nick. I won't let you!" Lindy pushed frantically at her door, but it was jammed by all the dirt. She began struggling out the car window, tears scalding her cheeks. She had to rescue her owls—please, please, before it was too late!

The bulldozer clanged abruptly to a halt just before it reached the first burrow. Lindy stared at Nick. He was sitting there in the bulldozer, not moving, not doing anything. Just sitting. She couldn't read his expression from here, but there was something about the rigid stillness of his posture that made her remain exactly where she was. She was trembling all over as she waited for him to make his next move.

Once again he surprised her. He switched off the engine and swung down from the bulldozer. Then he strode toward the onlookers. Several signs were being waved belligerently throughout the crowd: PROTECT THE HELPLESS! SAVE OUR BURROWS! DOWN WITH ALDRIDGE AVIATION! Lindy squeezed the rest of the way out her window and jogged after Nick.

He had reached Juliet by then. Taking her by the arm, he swiveled around and propelled her in a path back toward the bulldozer. Lindy stayed close behind the two of them.

"We need to talk where there's privacy," Nick said to Juliet, his voice steely.

"Of course, Romeo. That's fine with me." Juliet sounded cheerful, snuggling closer to him. Then she glanced over her shoulder at Lindy. "I believe Nicholas mentioned something about privacy, MacAllister. In other words, beat it."

But Lindy stayed right on their heels. Nick led Juliet to the foxhole, then turned and confronted her. His eyes were a hard, brilliant blue.

"Okay, it's gone on long enough. It's finished. We're not building the factory here."

Lindy's heart began to pound in wild hope. Could it be possible? Nick coming over to her side at last!

Juliet took a step toward him. "Romeo, this has to be a joke. What's the punch line?"

"This is no joke. I'm telling you exactly the way things are. Aldridge Aviation will not build a factory here. It's wrong." He started pacing back and forth in the foxhole. "I've tried to tell myself over and over it *isn't* wrong. I've used logic and reason to defend Aldridge . . . to defend myself. But when I started charging around in that crazy bulldozer, I realized all the logic in the world can't change the irrational truth. This place belongs to the owls. I can't fight that anymore. And neither can you, Juliet."

"You're actually going to listen to this . . . this person?" Juliet gestured scornfully at Lindy.

"Leave her out of it. This is between you and me now."

Lindy retreated a few feet, feeling that the battle no longer belonged to her. It belonged to Nick. He understood about the owls! A quiet happiness filled her, just knowing he had made this struggle his own.

Juliet gave the sash at her waist an angry yank. She was wearing yet another jumpsuit, a billowing, gauzy concoction in bright lime green. "All right, Nick, let's have it out. First of all, you promised me we'd build this factory."

"I don't take any promise lightly. But I have to do what's right. And so do you, Juliet. Choose another factory site. Or work with Ray on expanding the Meridian plant. In fact, I've been thinking about selling my share of the company to Ray. He'd make a good partner for you. I think we both realize it's time for a change at Aldridge."

"No. I want to work with *you*, Nick! Fine, we'll expand the factory in California. But there's no reason for you to sell out. I won't let you do it, not after everything we've been through together."

"It's time for me to move on. You know that's the truth."

"I have a say in this partnership. You can't go!"

Nick and Juliet faced each other like two big, angry Vikings. Nick was wearing one of his business shirts, but nothing could conceal his vibrant masculinity. His sleeves were pushed up haphazardly, revealing the strong muscles of his arms. His rumpled hair was amber-gold in the sunlight, as rich in color as a lion's fur. And the line of his jaw was clean, decisive...powerful.

As for Juliet, well, she was impressive, too, her magnificent curves outlined under that billowing gauze. She might easily have been a vengeful Nordic goddess descended from the sky on a green cloud. Lindy wouldn't have been surprised to see lightning bolts crackling out from Juliet's fingers.

And yet, Juliet's power seemed to be wavering a bit; there was almost a pleading in her voice when she spoke next.

"Dammit, Nick, you care more about some lousy owls than you do about me! You care more about Linden MacAllister."

"I told you, this doesn't have anything to do with Lindy. I've made my own decision."

"The hell it doesn't have anything to do with her! If you hadn't met her, if you'd never seen her . . . you and I, Nick . . . we'd be together."

He shook his head, but there was a gentleness in his eyes as he regarded Juliet. "We started out as such good friends. You've been trying to make us into something else. It can't work. Come on—accept it, Juliet. You knew we couldn't be more than friends a long time before I met Lindy."

Juliet's round cheeks seem to have deflated, like two balloons that no longer had the energy to hold air. "So that's all we were supposed to be, Nicholas? Buddies?"

"We're friends, Juliet. Nothing more."

"Yeah, sure. I should be grateful we had that much, right?" The bitterness in Juliet's voice was naked. Darn it all, Lindy didn't want to feel sorry for the woman! But she knew what Juliet was going through. She knew that for herself a platonic friendship with Nick would never, ever be enough.

As if sensing Lindy's sympathy and hating it, Juliet straightened her shoulders and tossed back her frizzy hair. She was dignified now.

"We *were* good friends for a very long time, Nick. I can't forget that. And you're the best person I've ever worked with. I have to respect you enough to accept your decision. No factory will be built on this spot." Juliet turned and gave Lindy a brittle smile. "So you win after all, Linden. How about that? Must feel pretty good."

"It's not about winning," Lindy said quietly. "It's about protecting the owls."

Juliet laughed, and the sound of her laughter was as bold and triumphant as ever. "You like winning as much as anybody else, MacAllister. You just won't admit it. At least I'm honest. I'll tell you up front that I can't stand to lose. Makes me madder than anything. Makes me want all the revenge I can have." She turned back to Nick. "So hear this, my good old buddy. As of this moment, we are officially no longer friends. I do believe I *will* accept a partnership with Ray Silverstein. We'll make Aldridge Aviation bigger and more successful than ever. You'll be sorry you left. Goodbye, Nick."

It was a grand speech, almost disguising Juliet's hurt. Almost, but not quite. Still regal, she wheeled in her billowing green cloud and marched back across the mesa. Her proud, adamant stride conveyed the distinct impression that she was invincible—and that, in future games, she was going to beat the heck out of all her opponents.

"WHEE-whee-whee-whee-whee!" scolded the sentry owl. Lindy craned her neck and saw the owl perched at the very top of the bulldozer. He gazed back at her, his yellow eyes unblinking and quite disapproving. He seemed to be telling her he'd already seen far too many humans for one day.

"Don't worry," she whispered. "We're leaving now. And you're safe at last."

NICK AND LINDY stood underneath a bower of the most atrocious plastic flowers—waxy roses an improbable shade of pink, all intertwined with garish daffodils. But Lindy didn't mind the fake flowers at all. She was leaning her head blissfully against Nick's chest, listening to the rumble of his voice as he spoke to her.

"I'll make a pilot out of you yet, Professor. You were a lot better on this flight."

"Well, maybe it helped that I didn't eat any of your cooking before we took off. But I almost turned Finola upside down, Nick! I think you'd better stay in charge of the controls."

"I can always tell a woman who was born to fly—even if she likes rocks more than airplanes. By the way, tell me how you like the sound of this—the Linden MacAllister Nature Preserve."

She shifted her head. "Nick, what are you talking about?"

"Before Juliet left for St. Louis yesterday, I signed papers to buy the factory site from Aldridge Aviation. Every last owl burrow."

Lindy threw her arms around Nick and hugged him fiercely. "Oh, thank you. Thank you! Now the owls will always be safe. Only let's call it the Jarrett-MacAllister Preserve."

"Done. But there's something else I may have neglected to tell you before. I love you, Lindy. It took me a little while to figure that out, but I finally did." His voice was husky, and he seemed to like saying these words to her. He said them again. "Lord, I do love you, Professor."

She raised her hands to his face, filled with joyful amazement that love was being returned to her in such full measure. Nick's skin was scratchy to her touch, for he was growing out his beard again. By now she'd discovered that anything he did with his jaw was fine with her. She ran her fingers through his silky, golden brown hair. Why, any day now it would be time for him to pay another visit to Fred the Barber. Lindy accidentally bumped Nick's safari hat, tilting it at an odd angle. He looked rakish and irresistible. She kissed him, there underneath the pink plastic roses.

Several kisses later they broke apart for breath, but still held on to each other.

"Nick, I love you so much I don't know what to do," Lindy said unsteadily. "But how will it all work out? You can't stand dinky little towns out in the middle of nowhere, and—"

"Now and then one of those dinky little towns has a tendency to grow on a person. And I've decided to hire you as my site consultant for Jarrett Aviation."

"I accept! I can't wait to see the first airplane you design."

"The Jarrett Owl, you mean? Hey, you can be my test pilot."

Lindy smiled and breathed in Nick's wonderful minty scent. "I feel like I'm flying twenty feet above the ground this very minute, that's how happy I am.

I'm even glad you brought me here to Las Vegas to show me the Happy Blossom Wedding Chapel. I guess you could say this place has been a turning point in your life," she added wryly. "Well, now we've seen it. What do you want to do next?"

"Get married, of course. Last time I came here with the wrong woman. Today I'm here with the perfect one. I don't want to waste any time." He gazed solemnly at his watch. "The way I figure it, there's only about sixty seconds left of our twenty-four-hour agreement. I want to renew the lease. How about a hundred years together?" '

Lindy stared at him. "But, Nick, I didn't think... Get married? Are you serious? You really want—"

He grinned. "Slow down, Professor. That toreador inside the chapel only needs to hear two words from you. 'I do.' After that it's simple. We already have a good start on a family—you, me and the yellow wonder dog."

"Hammersmith loves you almost as much as I do. He really does." Lindy patted her tangled hair. She was going to make a rather odd bride in her corduroy pants and hiking boots, a battered Dodgers baseball cap instead of a veil. And Nick certainly would not be the most conventional groom in his blue jeans, chukka boots and safari hat. But Lindy wouldn't have changed a single detail. She put her hand in Nick's.

"I'm ready," she said. "In fact, I have our honeymoon all planned out. How does Carlsbad Caverns sound to you?"

He chuckled. "Sounds great. I'll spend any amount of time in caves, as long as you're there with me."

"Well, let's hurry up and get married, then!"

A few moments later Nick and Lindy stood hand in hand at the altar of the Happy Blossom Wedding Chapel. Over the altar a large neon heart blinked and gave off a strange buzzing noise. It wasn't exactly a melodious sound, but it made Lindy as happy as any wedding march. Surrounding the red neon heart were more garlands of fake roses and daffodils. A young man dressed as a toreador had given Lindy one of the plastic roses to tuck behind her ear. Now the toreador fiddled with his cape, a truly impressive garment of red and gold silk. It wasn't clear if the ceremony had started yet, but Nick had already tucked his hat under one arm, and certainly the witnesses were in place: a woman studiously plucking lint off her pants and an elderly man in jogging shorts.

At last the toreador began thumbing through a dog-eared book. "Do you, Linden Eloise MacAllister, take this man to be your lawfully wedded husband, to have and to hold, from this day forward, as long as you both shall live?" He made an exuberant swirl with his cape. Lindy didn't know whether she was expected to say "I do" or charge under the toreador's cape like a bull.

"I do," she declared, giving Nick's hand a vigorous squeeze.

The toreador eyed Nick. "Do you, Nicholas Jarrett, take this woman to be your lawfully wedded wife, to have and to hold, from this day forward, as long as you both shall live?" He made another pass with his cape.

"I do." Nick gave Lindy's hand an answering squeeze.

"I now pronounce you . . . No, wait. The rings. Do you have the rings?"

"Lord, I forgot all about that." Nick looked disturbed, but the elderly man in jogging shorts sprang into action. He scuttled over to one of the benches, grabbed a leather case and flashed it open in front of Lindy and Nick.

"Rings," he announced. "Take your pick—all kinds, all sizes."

It was a wonderful and bewildering array of jewelry. Lindy picked out a simple gold band, and Nick found one to match. She held up her hand and admired her wedding ring. It looked just right on her finger. She knew she would cherish it always.

The toreador slapped his book shut, giving a final flourish of his cape. "I now pronounce you husband and wife!"

"Hey, aren't you forgetting something?" Nick demanded.

The toreador opened his book again and peered anxiously inside it. "Oh, yes. You may now kiss the bride."

But Nick was already kissing Lindy for all he was worth, gathering her close in his arms. After a moment they broke apart, both of them laughing and breathless. The neon heart buzzed. The elderly man in jogging shorts did a few deep knee bends. The woman stopped picking lint off her pants and clapped shyly. It was difficult to tell if she was applauding the old man's limber knees, or the fact that Lindy had just married Nick. Altogether, it was the most beautiful wedding in the world. Lindy smiled and gave her husband another kiss. Oh, she liked the sound of those words: her husband, Nick Jarrett.

The man she loved. The man she would love all the rest of her life.

OVER THE YEARS, TELEVISION HAS BROUGHT
THE LIVES AND LOVES OF MANY CHARACTERS INTO
YOUR HOMES. NOW HARLEQUIN INTRODUCES YOU
TO THE TOWN AND PEOPLE OF

One small town—twelve terrific love stories.

GREAT READING... GREAT SAVINGS...
AND A FABULOUS FREE GIFT!

Each book set in Tyler is a self-contained love story; together, the
twelve novels stitch the fabric of the community.

By collecting proofs-of-purchase found in each Tyler book, you can
receive a fabulous gift, ABSOLUTELY FREE! And use our special
Tyler coupons to save on your next TYLER book purchase.

Join us for the fifth TYLER book,
BLAZING STAR by Suzanne Ellison, available in July.

Is there really a murder cover-up?
Will Brick and Karen overcome differences and find true love?

HARLEQUIN
Romance®

Coming Next Month

#3205 FIREWORKS! Ruth Jean Dale
Question: What happens when two blackmailing grandfathers coerce a
dashing rodeo cowboy and his estranged Boston-society wife into spending
time together in Hell's Bells, Texas? Answer: *Fireworks!*

#3206 BREAKING THE ICE Kay Gregory
When hunky Brett Jackson reenters Sarah's life after ten years, he brings a
young son, two dogs and a ferret. His questionable reputation comes, too—
which doesn't make him the kind of guy for whom an ice maiden should melt....

#3207 MAN OF TRUTH Jessica Marchant
Sent to Switzerland to promote a new vacation package, Sally has no idea
she'll have to confront Kemp Whittaker. Film producer, TV presenter, nature
lover and every woman's fantasy, he opposes Sally and everything she stands
for. Can she withstand his assault?

#3208 A KIND OF MAGIC Betty Neels
Fergus Cameron's arrogance makes him the kind of man most women find
annoying, and Rosie is no exception. Admittedly, he can be charming when it
suits him—not that it matters to her. Fergus has already told her he's found
the girl he's going to marry.

#3209 FAR FROM OVER Valerie Parv
Jessie knows that no matter how hard she tries, there's no way to stop
Adrian Cole from coming back into her life. She knows she wants a second
chance with him—but she's afraid of his reaction to her son, Sam.

#3210 BOTH OF THEM Rebecca Winters
Bringing home the wrong baby—it's got to be a one-in-a-billion chance. Yet
Cassie Arnold's sister, Susan, believed it had happened to her. With Susan's
tragic death, Cassie's obliged to continue her sister's investigation. And she
discovers, to her shock, that Susan was right; her real nephew is living with
divorced Phoenix banker Trace Ramsey, as his son. When Trace becomes
aware of the truth, he insists on having *both* children. There's only one
solution, he says—Cassie will have to marry him....
Both of Them is the third title in The Bridal Collection.

AVAILABLE THIS MONTH:

#3199 A CINDERELLA AFFAIR
Anne Beaumont

#3200 WILD TEMPTATION
Elizabeth Duke

#3201 BRAZILIAN ENCHANTMENT
Catherine George

#3202 LOVE YOUR ENEMY
Ellen James

#3203 RUNAWAY FROM LOVE
Jessica Steele

#3204 NEW LEASE ON LOVE
Shannon Waverly

Back by Popular Demand

Janet Dailey®
Americana

A romantic tour of America through fifty favorite Harlequin
Presents, each set in a different state researched by Janet
and her husband, Bill. A journey of a lifetime in one
cherished collection.

In July, don't miss the exciting states featured in:

Title   **#35 OHIO**
        The Widow and the Wastrel
        #36 OKLAHOMA
        Six White Horses